STICKS AND STONES

about the author

Susan Price has been writing for as long as she can remember. At fourteen she entered and won the *Daily Mirror* short story competition and at sixteen she wrote *The Devil's Piper*, a fantasy which was published just after she left school. She has now written many other books, including *Twopence a Tub*, *From Where I Stand* and, most recently, a collection of her own tales, *Crack A Story*. *The Ghost Drum* won the 1987 Library Association Carnegie Medal for an outstanding children's book.

Apart from writing, Susan has worked as a box-humper in a retail warehouse, a guide in the open-air Black Country museum, and for two days as a dish-washer. 'As a dish-washer,' she says, 'I was a complete failure.'

She lives in Tividale, in the West Midlands.

by the same author

GHOSTS AT LARGE
FROM WHERE I STAND
IN A NUTSHELL
THE CARPENTER AND OTHER STORIES
CHRISTOPHER UPTAKE
THE DEVIL'S PIPER
HERE LIES PRICE
CRACK A STORY

Faber Children's Paperbacks
THE GHOST DRUM
HOME FROM HOME
TWOPENCE A TUB

STICKS AND STONES
Susan Price

faber and faber
LONDON · BOSTON

First published in Great Britain in 1976
by Faber and Faber Limited
3 Queen Square London WC1N 3AU
This paperback edition first published in 1992

Printed in Great Britain by
Cox & Wyman Ltd, Reading, Berkshire

© Susan Price, 1976

A CIP record for this book is available from the
British Library.

ISBN: 0-571-16315-7

1

The firm's own soap-powders were on special offer, and the Gaffer wanted a big display of 'em. There was a skip-load of 'em upstairs, he said, all ready to bring down and stack. So I left the office and bounded up the stairs, two at a time, into the stock-room, a big, chilly, gloomy place, divided into tunnels by walls of boxes and shelves. Now, half-way up the Toiletries and Tinned Fruit aisle, I saw a pair of long, slim, smooth legs, ending in these high-heeled, ankle-strapped black shoes. The blood started circulating again at the sight of 'em, spirits to rise, the interest started to seep back into life. I sped up the aisle, like, and found the owner of the pair of legs sitting on a box of tinned rhubarb, sheltered behind a stack of sliced cling peaches. Vicky.

I forgot about soap-powder for the moment. From the day I started work and first saw Victoria Wallace, I've fancied her. She has her faults – I've counted 'em off time and time again. She's not perfect, like all those pin-up girls in the photos under me bed. Her face's a bit puddingy and sour until she smiles, her's got a double chin, and the occasional pimple – but her's also got a real curvy figure, and great legs, and best of all – she's real. She's not in a photo. She's sitting on a box of rhubarb right in front of me, displaying yards of leg.

There's just one snag. A photo's however you want her. I

can have a photo of some film-actress, and the more I look at it, the more she thinks I'm fantastic and everything, and it don't matter that she's as old as me Mom (although a lot better-looking). But Vicky, who's real, and only about three years older than me, just isn't interested.

"Hello, Vick, what you doin'?" I asked. She didn't answer, so I bent over her to see what she was writing on the cardboard tray in her hand. She was playing noughts and crosses against herself. "What you doin', you naughty girl? Get your behind smacked." And if she'd lift it up a bit, I'd be only too glad to do the smacking.

She sighed. "Oh-h – go away, Graeme."

This put me off, and I straightened up to lean against the cling peaches. I thought of another approach and stooped down again. "What you up here for anyway?"

She slapped the cardboard down on her knee, making all her thigh wobble. I was tempted to make it wobble again, but she'd only get mad. She said, "This skip's got to go downstairs." There was a skip in the aisle by her, packed and piled high with boxes of tins. "It's all got to go on my fixture, but I can't move the thing." She tipped up her head and rolled back her eyes, chanting, "So I told the Gaffer and he said he'd come and move it for me, but he hasn't, so here I am, waiting. Satisfied?"

I was quick off the mark. "No need to wait for him. I'll take it down for you."

She gave me a look from the corners of her eyes, and crimped up one corner of her mouth. "You couldn't move it."

"*Bet* I could then!"

She stood up and shook out her hair, and said, "There's some of these peaches to go on anyway but they'm stacked too high, I can't get 'em." As if that settled the matter. She irritated me. What did she think *I* was – a drawing on the wall?

"I'll put 'em on for you."

"You couldn't reach." Which was a quick dig about my

8

height. So, all right, I'm only about five foot three – shorter than she is – so all right, I'm short and skinny, but I ain't helpless. "Don't you worry," I said. "I'll do it. Just you watch me."

I fetched a box of Malayan pineapple, dropped it by the peaches, and stepped up on top of it. I reached up, at full stretch, took a finger-tip hold on the top box.

"You'll never do it," she said confidently from below. "Hey – don't drop it on me!"

"I won't drop it on anybody," I said, a bit breathlessly. Scrabbling and tugging, I inched the box to the edge of the stack. A bit further and it tipped – I thought for a second it was going to flatten me. But I held it up and it came down slowly. I took the weight on my cheek and shoulder. My arms trembled and the strain dug painfully into my jaw and collar-bone. Hugging the box carefully I stepped down from the pineapple, staggered and tottered, and only the soap-powders against the far wall saved me from falling over.

"See!" Vicky crowed. "I *told* you you'd never manage it. Come here, I'll give you hand."

"No need, there's no need," I said angrily, turning the box away from her. "It was only getting down off there, it's no trouble now. No – you'd only get in the way. I can manage. It ain't heavy." Not half. I could feel the tendons or whatever in me shoulders parting.

Vick stood back, annoyed, her hands on her hips. She looked really smashin' like that, her pink overall pinched in to her waist. Smashin'. "You've still got to get it on the skip, you know."

"Yeh, I know, I know! I can do it." I wedged the box against the skip, taking some of the weight off me arms and preparing meself for the big boost. I got me hands beneath the box and hoisted it on to me shoulder. I gritted me teeth so that I wouldn't gasp while she was watching me. I bent at the knees and shoved upwards. The box teetered on the edge of the skip, and then I shoved it over. "There you are!" I said.

9

"How many do you want?"

"Three," she said, deadpan.

Ah well. I'd been hoping she only wanted the one, but I hopped back on to the pineapple as if this was all I'd ever wanted to do, all me life. She watched me without offering any help, but her eyes were as hard as nails. Scornful, you know. Folded arms. I nearly killed meself putting them two other boxes on the skip, but she wouldn't be impressed.

I pushed hair that was slightly damp out of my eyes and asked, "You want it took down?" Just look at that lad, all that he can do, and still wants to do more – never tired . . . she had to be impressed sooner or later.

"No need to bother," she said.

"No bother," I said. "Won't take me half a minute."

"The Gaffer'll be coming up in a minute to fetch it for me."

"I'll take it down now, so you won't have to wait," I said.

"*Graeme* – I don't *want* it took down – !" This was in the manner of a desperate scream as I swung on the skip and started it moving. But I couldn't have stopped it for her then, however she pleaded, because if I'd stopped, it would have just carried on, run me down and crushed me. I heard her heels clipping on the floor as she ran after us – me and the skip. "Ooh, Graeme, you am a pest! I was just havin' a quiet sit-down – "

I dodged from behind the skip before it smashed into the lift-doors. If the Gaffer had seen that I'd have copped out. "We have to have the painters in every fortnight with you around," he'd say. "Take it slow, I've told you." But you have to pull hard to start one of them skips, and once you've started it, they get faster by theirselves. I slid the doors of the lift aside, and went around the skip to push it in. It stuck against the lift-floor which, like all the other floors in this place, wasn't level. I set my back against the skip and pushed with my feet.

Harry, the butcher, looked out of his butcher's shop. "All

10

right, Gray? Want hand?"

"No, no, it's all right, Harry. I've got it, it'll go in a minute." No chance, but I hate being helped.

Vicky was acting very bored and hoity-toity. Shook out her hair. "He can't move it. Thinks he's Tarzan. Why don't you leave it for the Gaffer? I never asked you to shift it in the first place."

"I can move it!" I went round to the front of the skip again, inside the lift, and tried to lift one wheel over the step and into the lift with me. But there was just too much weight on it. I took hold of the skip and swung on it, bending at the knees and swinging low. The opposite corner of the skip swung away from the lift. "Bloody Hell!"

"Language," Vicky said.

I took hold of both sides of the skip and threw myself backwards on them, cracking my neck. I gritted my teeth and pulled until my fingers slipped and sent me flying back. I wrestled the skip, shaking it from side to side. I yanked and yanked at one side, then the other. I sweated and panted and rubbed my hands raw, and it wouldn't move one bloody millimetre.

"What's goin' on here?" the Gaffer's voice said. He always talks to you and treats you as if you're about three years old. I suppose it's his being so big. He is a big bloke, tall and broad. Makes me feel as useless as a plastic gnome. I suppose when you're that big you do look down on people. Wish I had the chance. Anyway, his head and shoulders, his big ugly mush, appeared over the top of the skip. "Oh," he said, nodding, "it's Gray. He's fightin' like a tiger here. What for?"

As if he couldn't see what for. "I *told* him to leave it," Vicky said.

"I'll have it in in a minute," I said.

"Never in a million years, Gray," the Gaffer said. He squeezed into the lift with me, through a space I would have walked through like a door. "Let's see – it's too big for thee, Gray, that's why. You'll rupture yourself the way you go on.

11

I couldn't move this by meself. When you've got a skip as loaded as this, you ask somebody to give you hand, all right? You could have asked Harry."

I looked sulky, I knew I was looking sulky. I hate being helped. It gets up me nose like pepper. Makes me look a fool.

"It's stuck against the lift," the Gaffer said. Wonderful. As if I didn't know that. He said, "Get the other side, Gray – now, when I say 'pull' – you pull." He crouched down and took hold of the skip just above the wheel, leaned back, grunted, "Pull!" and I pulled, and one corner of the skip lurched into the lift. We changed ends and repeated the process. "There you are," the Gaffer said. I thought he was going to pat me on the head. As if I couldn't have moved it myself. I could have – eventually. "Now – Vicky can go down and do some work, and young Graeme here can go and get that soap-powder like I told him."

"I was goin' to take it down and push it over to the fruit for her," I said.

The Gaffer pointed to the stock-room. I went.

"It wouldn't have took me long to push it over there, Gaffer," I said, walking backwards as he followed me into the stock-room.

"No, but the fun and games round the tinned fruit afterwards would. There's plenty of folk down there can move it for her." Then he rubbed his nose with one finger and said, "Mind, her's a cracker."

I found the skip of soap-powders and swung back on it to start it rolling.

"Can you manage that, Gray?"

"Yeah, yeah." It was true this time. Soap-powders aren't quite as heavy as tins, although salt, flour and sugar are heavier.

"Oh Gray – " he called after me as I shoved the skip out on to the landing. I went back to see what he wanted. "Are you on tonight?"

Well, see, it was Friday, and Bancroft's stay open from

12

half-eight in the morning to nine at night on Fridays. But the staff, excepting the Gaffer, only works one Friday night in three. Wednesday is half-day closing, and if you work Wednesday morning, you knock off at five on Friday and one on Saturday. Then the next week, you work till six on Saturday and have Wednesday off and knock off at five on Friday; and the week after that you have Wednesday off, finish at one on Saturday again, but work till nine Friday. I said, "No, Gaffer; I worked Wednesday."

"Oh," he said. "Oh. Well, you'd better do them stock-cards this afternoon then, you know the ones – they got to be done."

"Right you are." I turned to go, but he called me back. "Gray – how's the lessons?"

He meant the Management Course I'm taking. You get these lessons through the post every month.

"Fine," I said, "all right." But, I thought, it was no good. I pushed my fringe out of my eyes and back over my head with one hand. "Ah – 'cept for the percentage thingies."

He stopped and stared at me. "What about 'em, Gray?"

"The percentages and profits. I can't do 'em, I don't understand it. I asked me Dad, but he can't either."

"Have you got it with you?"

"No, sir."

"Ah – well – bring 'em tomorrow, bring 'em up to the office and I'll see if I can't explain 'em."

"Yessir." Backing off, I added uneasily, "Er – thanks, sir." I went hurriedly back to the skip, and pressed the button to call the lift up. I shoved the skip into the lift – the lift-floor had stopped below the landing this time – and slammed the two doors, whined down to the shop floor.

I shoved through the swing doors into the shop. As I was passing the fruit counter, Mrs. Harris called me. I left the skip and sloped over to her. "What have I done now?"

She's a big fat Welsh lady, must be about forty. "Oh yes, you've always done something wrong, we know. Showing off, were you, upstairs?" She pulled me closer to her by my shoulder, and whispered warmly in my ear, "You're showing off to the wrong one, my lamb. She's taken, is our Vicky."

"Well, I could take her back, couldn't I?" I said.

She smiled. "What I want you for is to ask you, do you want some orange, because we've got some bruised oranges here." She laid an orange on the counter and neatly cut off the bruised part.

I grabbed for the biggest part. "I'll have that."

She banged the blunt edge of the knife on my knuckles. "Oh no, you won't, my boy. That's for Mr. Pritchard. You have that piece." She offered me another slice, skewered on the end of the knife.

"That's the smallest," I said. She bellied menacingly up to me. "Are you going to argue then, you little squirt?"

"Who d'you think you are? Cassius Clay? I could flatten you," I said.

"Mr. Pritchard, he says he's going to flatten me." Mr. Clarence Pritchard was coming in from the back with a box of spring-cabbage. His name really is Clarence. I call him Claz. I began calling him Mr. Claz when I wanted something between respect and friendliness, but I dropped the 'Mr.' after a bit. Claz's my mate, Claz is. On my very first day at work, he said, "Come and work for me a bit," gave me something to do, made me feel useful. Now he just sniggered. He sniggers quite a lot. He's little, littler even than me, and snuffly and grubby-looking. He gives me lessons in female anatomy. I began to suck at my piece of orange, and to lick up the juice running down my wrist, while Mrs. Harris cut up another.

"Am you feedin' him our oranges again?" Claz asked.

"Oranges am good for you," said Mrs. Rita Harris firmly. "Lots of vitamins in them. They'll make him grow up big and strong."

"Cheek," I said. Claz sniggered and punched me in the ribs. Mrs. Harris gave Claz his share of the oranges she'd cut up, and piled a little mound of orange slices in front of me.

14

Claz put a whole slice into his mouth, peel and all, then took my hand and put the rest of his share into it, below the counter, where Mrs. Harris couldn't see. I grinned at him, and put the whole sticky lot into my overall pocket.

"You come and help me when Reet goes to her dinner, Gramey?" Claz asked. I wished he wouldn't call me 'Gramey'. I nodded. "Sure." The lift whined down from upstairs. "That's the Gaffer!" I said, and scooped up my orange from the counter, went to put it in my pocket. "Don't put it in your pocket!" Mrs. Harris said. "It'll get all dirty and fluffy."

"I like fluff," I said, and went back to the skip before the Gaffer came. I pushed it over to where the display was to be set up, but took my time about starting. I yawned and scratched my head, rubbed my eyes. I was in no hurry. I mean, once you've stacked one box, you've stacked them all. You get a bit browned-off. The Gaffer wanted 'em finished by dinner-time. I opened a box, and fetched the price-tape and priced them, and I stacked them up, layer after layer. I yawned and looked at my watch. Five past eleven. Roll on twelve. Or, better still, five o'clock.

I don't like this job much. I like the people. I like the Gaffer, he's a nice bloke, even if he does talk down and make me feel about two inches high. I like old Claz all right. I like all the old ladies, like Mrs. Harris, who make a fuss over me because I'm the youngest on the staff. And I certainly like all the girls – but I'm not so strong on the job. Everything I do, almost, I could do without thinking, and that means I have to think of something else, which is fine if you have something else. If you haven't, you get bored.

Dad keeps saying it'll be better when I've passed the exams, and I'm qualified to be a manager, but that ain't all the training you get. That just gets you ready for the next stage, if you're chosen for that. After I pass the exam, if I pass, I'll still be a sixteen-year-old kid, and I'll be stuck with stacking soap-powders. I might never get a job as a manager.

15

Or I might just be a department manager, like Claz. I bet I could do his job now. He only makes out his order and sells the stuff. I could guess how many lettuces he'll need as well as he can, I bet.

I opened another box and thumbed the price-stickers from the tape on to the packets. Then piled another layer on the stack. Yawned. I'd never wanted this job. Only I'd left school and had no job to go to. The Labour sent me after two jobs I didn't get, and then Dad came home and said he'd rung up the manager of Bancroft's, the supermarket, and I was to go the next day for an interview. It took me about ten minutes to get the job and I've been here ever since. I never fancied it – I mean, working in a supermarket, with a white cotton overall, and a big 'B' and an 'S' embroidered on the pocket in red – a white overall – but I couldn't go on sponging off Mom and Dad. I had to get a job. And after I'd got it – well – Dad don't approve of people who keep changing their jobs. He don't like it. They're insecure, he says, people who can't face up to reality – how'd you like that? He talks like that when he's drunk. They can't settle down, he says, and hold a job. Well, he says that, and I know what he means. I know I'd better not get any ideas about changing my job.

The stack went up another two layers and I yawned again. I'm always yawning at work, I always feel sleepy. The air's stale, see, and the place is gloomy, there's no windows anywhere except in the staff-room and right down at the front of the shop. I don't work down there very often. Where I work, up at the other end, if they switch the lights out at mid-day, it's pitch-black. And the building's all concrete and tiles; it's cold. Like being buried alive eight hours a day. You forget what daylight's like and you're surprised when you go out on the night. And then you get this miserable feeling that it'll be dark soon and all the day's gone while you've been shut up in there, and that all your life's going the same way – in working. I've been feeling worse and worse about this lately. Must be advancing age. I'll be seventeen in – just over ten months' time.

I finished the stack and stood back from it, to have room to really stretch and yawn. I looked at my watch. Five to twelve. I went over to the dairy fridge and spent five minutes regimenting the cheeses and cream cartons, pretending to be working. The second me watch finger touched twelve, I was into the back and pelting up the stairs two at a time, swinging wide from the banister at the landing and crashing straight into the Gaffer, who stopped me like a brick wall. "Hold on, hold on," he said, pushing me away. "What's the hurry?"

"'S twelve," I said.

Keeping me back with one hand, he looked at his watch. "It still wants a minute."

"Not by my watch, Gaffer."

"Ah, well, you've got one of them special watches that gains as the day goes on – I know. And you was late again this morning, so – "

"I wasn't late! Dead on half – "

"You was at the *door* by half-past eight, but it was twenty to nine by the time you was down here, overall on and working. You'm supposed to be workin' by half-eight, not taking your coat off. So you owe me ten minutes, and you can just hang on until I reckon it's time for you to go." Vicky and Brenda passed on their way up to their dinners. "Oh, Gaffer – "I said.

"I've told you about running up these stairs, anyway," the Gaffer said. "Running up like that, not looking where you're going. What if it had been Mrs. Harris or Winnie you ran into and not me? You'd have knocked 'em flyin'. A menace to them around you, you are, my lad. All right, go on, get out me sight."

I jumped past him and pelted up the stairs, two at a time.

"GRAEME!"

I stopped and stood still for a second. Then I looked down and said, "Sorry, Gaffer." I walked slowly up, as slow as

17

Claz does when the lift's broke down and he has to use the stairs. As soon as I was at the top and out of sight I banged back the door leading to the staff-room, raced down the dark corridor, past the 'Female Persons' Toilet' and the 'Male Persons' Toilet', slammed back the staff-room door, and was dazzled by the daylight.

"Cor," I said. I went and stood on a chair, opened a window and leaned out. "It's a smashin' day."

Winnie – that's right, Winnie – the tea lady sighed dismally. "Yes, Graeme, love, it is, ain't it?"

Brenda and Vicky weren't there. They must be in the Female Persons' Toilet, prinking up their female persons with lip-stick and such. I said, "It is! I think I'm goin' out."

I had been going to eat me sandwiches up here, but now I thought I'd go to the park. You can see the park from the staff-room, it's just across the road, behind the shop. The grass was so green, it looked new painted, and the daffodils were out tra-la. The fountain was a-going away there and I could see a gardener modging about in one of the flower-beds. One of my mates, that gardener. So I stripped off me overall, revealing, ta-da, me tatty old purple jumper that I've had since I was twelve, and trousers nearly as old. I haven't grown very much since then, see, and I've got skinnier, so they still fitted more or less. I could see Winnie didn't think a lot of me ensemble-like, so I decided to get out before the others could pass judgement. I took me sandwiches out me jacket pocket and ran back downstairs. I went out through the loading door, past the big notice which says, 'Any member of staff found entering or leaving the premises by this door will be subject to instant dismissal.' I jumped off the loading step, landing with knees bent and palms on the ground. I went out through the gap in the wall where the lorries come in, crossed the road and climbed over the railings into the park. Going round to the gate would be wasting my dinner-time. I ran across the grass to the centre bed where the fountain is. The gardener was there, crouching down to

18

plant seedlings. I bent over him and the fountain splattered on me too. "Hello, Gaffer."

He looked up. "Hello, Youth. Ain't seen you for a week or two, have I?"

I shook my head. "What you puttin' in, then?"

"Polyanthus these am, Blossom."

"Polyanthus!" I went down on my knees. The seedlings were planted in them little pots made of peat. "Can I put some in?"

He grinned and dozens of wrinkles fanned out from his eyes and around his mouth. "Ar – go on."

I dug a hole with my hand. "All right, all right," the old gaffer said. "Don't go through to Australia. Make it big enough to take the pot . . . all right, now put your pot in, make it comfortable." He watched in silence as I planted a couple more. "Keep it neat. Remember, they've got to make a neat line when they flower . . . Like flowers, do you?"

I took a minute before answering. I was always careful about admitting that I liked flowers. If you say something like that, people wave their hands and say, "Oh, *do* you, sweetie?" or summat. But he was a gardener hisself. "Yeah, I like flowers a bit – yeh, I like flowers. I like seein' 'em come up from seeds, an' waitin' for 'em to flower. It's like waitin' for your birthday, or Christmas – I got a cactus is goin' to flower."

"Keep the garden at home, I suppose, do you?"

"We ain't got a garden," I said. "We live in a flat. Fifteen floors up." I firmed the earth around another seedling with my knuckles. "I got this cactus in a pot, an' a Busy Lizzie I give to me mother in the kitchen, but I have to keep an eye on it because her either don't water it for a month or tries to drown it. An' I've got these marigolds planted in a grape-box under me bed, but I don't know what I'm goin' to do with 'em when they need pottin'; an' a date-palm an' a grape-vine, an' this plant smells like lemons when you squeeze the leaves."

19

He snorted. "Sounds like a bloody zoological garden, your house."

I grinned. "Me mom don't like it. Her says the dirt gets everywhere. I'd have pots on the balcony, but her won't let me. Says they'd get in her way. Her don't like the balcony, see, her's scared of heights. So when her's got to hang clothes out or anythin', her likes to run out an' run in. Her says her wouldn't be able to if it was full of pots."

"I never knowed a mother agree with anythin'," he said, showing a great understanding of mothers. I could almost believe he'd had a mother himself, once.

"We used to have a garden, at the old house. Used to have daffodils an' roses. But we left there when I was six or so. I can remember the daffodils, though."

"I wouldn't like to live in a flat," he said. He bedded three seedlings in the time it took me to put one in. I did a couple more.

"You'm a one." I looked round and he was watching me, his hands on his knees. "You knock off for your dinner, come out here and do my work for me. You'm as daft as you am high."

I know I'm not very tall. There's no need for everybody to keep rubbing it in. "Well, that's not very daft, is it?" I said.

He grinned. "You'll do, blossom." He shifted and creakingly sat down on the grass. "What time is it?"

"Nearly quarter past twelve."

"Right, well, if you'll fetch me jacket from over there, I'll have me dinner. Your legs am younger than mine."

That's what everybody says. But I went and fetched his jacket for him, and he took out his parcel of sandwiches, wrapped in bread-paper. "Cold egg. Want one?"

"No ta, I've got mine here. Cheese."

He filled his face with cold egg, sighed and leaned back on one elbow, while I sat upright and cross-legged, like the Buddha in the antique shop up the road. "How's the job then?"

"Oh, it's all right," I said. "There's worse. I been pilin' soap-powders all this mornin'. Did some balin' early on."

He hissed between his teeth, shaking his head. "Oh, that sounds like borin' work to me."

"No! 'S all right." I pulled me knees up to me shoulders and held me ankles, while I thought about what I'd just said. I'd just said it like automatically, because he'd said I must be bored. But it wasn't exactly true, and he was a mate, so I began to put the picture right. "I do get a bit fed up some-times. It's all sort of shut-in, see. It's dark – all electric light. Makes your eyes tired."

He chewed his egg sandwiches, looking up at the fountain. "What you want is a job in the open."

"Yeah," I said doubtfully.

He pressed his chin down on his chest, giving himself a concertina of double-chins, and looked at me along his length. "Wouldn't you like to work outside, then?"

"Well – yeah – I would . . . I wouldn't know what to do."

"What you mean, you wouldn't know what to do?"

"Well – I wouldn't want to work on a building-site – that'd be as bad as stacking soap-powders – an' – well, what else is there."

He sat up suddenly. "God strewth, the kid wants coal cracking on his head!" he said. "There ain't only brickies work outside, you know – I work outside, don't I? What about farm-labourers, and foresters – an' dustmen for God's sake, and street-sweepers!"

"Yeah," I said, "but you'm a gardener."

He stared at me a minute. Couldn't figure my thought processes. "I *know* I'm a gardener. What's that got to do with it?"

"Well – I couldn't get a job as a gardener."

"Why not? Have you got greenfly?"

I rolled over on me back, laughing. "No – I don't think so – but, you know, I wouldn't know where to go or anything – an' you have to have 'O' levels, don't you?"

"I didn't – and you apply to the Department of Parks and Gardens. Or just go to the Labour and tell 'em you'd like to be a park-gardener – they'll help you out. I used to have assistant, but he left. Job's been open for months now. They don't like it, you see, these youngsters, the money's not much. You can earn more in any factory."

"Gardenin' – that'd be great." I thought of all the days like this, and hotter days. "I'd like that, I'd really like that."

He grinned. "Mind, it can be bloody cold, and it ain't so lovely when it bales down of rain."

"I like rain," I said quickly. "I ain't so keen on cold."

"Well," he said. "It's worth thinking about. If you don't like that job."

"I don't," I admitted. I stretched out full length on the grass, with all those yellow daffodils, and I thought about it. But then I came up on one elbow and beheaded a daisy with my thumbnail. "Me Dad wouldn't like it," I said.

"Why should he like it or not?"

"He just wouldn't," I said. "He don't like people to change their jobs. He'd stop me."

"He couldn't once you'm eighteen."

"That's two years."

"Ain't long to wait."

This gave me pause. Any man who could say two years wasn't long to wait wasn't like the sympathetic listener I'd taken him for. Two years. It was endless. I could be dead.

"And if you really want to be a gardener, I can't see your Dad stopping you," he said. Now he sounded like a teacher.

"Who said I wanted to be a gardener at all?" I came back with. He said nothing, but knew as well I did that I wanted to be a gardener.

"Yeah, I'd like to be."

"Well, you should talk to your Dad about it."

This had much the effect on my mind that the bombs had on Coventry. I retreated in disorder. "Twenty to one, better be gettin' back."

22

"At twenty to one?"

"Yeah, gotta go, tara." I ran across the grass, and waved from the top of the railings when he called, "Tara, Gray." I didn't know his name but he knew mine because he'd heard me called from Bancroft's.

I jumped up to sit on the loading step, stood up, and went in to run up the stairs to the staff-room. The air inside was heavy with faggots and peas, and they'd shut the window. There were only girls in there – Brenda and Vicky and Gwyn and Babs, all curly hair and eye make-up, cor, cor. I stalked in among them, a lion among doves. "Oh bloody hell, it's him," Vicky said, lighting up a fag, which I'm not allowed to smoke. (Dad would do his nut if he caught me smoking, or even suspected me.)

Vicky looked round at me again as she shook the match out. "You'm back early, aren't you?"

"I ain't like some folk, always late," I said.

"You must be daft, comin' back early."

I avoided Vicky, because she had learnt her repartee (as they say) in factories and always gave me worse than she got; and I swooped down on Brenda, who was smirking and smoking in aloof manner. "What you laughin' at?"

She blinked down her sexy purple eyelids for a minute, to remind me that she's eighteen, and blew out smoke before giving me a look like I was something the cat had dragged in and had chewed a bit first. "It's none of your business."

I swung round her chair so that it rocked and pulled away from the table, nearly throwing her off; and leaned down to say in her other ear, "I'll punch your head in a minute."

She jumped up to stop herself falling over as I pulled at her chair again, and grabbed at the chair-seat to straighten it. I rattled it about from leg to leg, twisting it out of her grip. "Oh bloody Graeme!"

"Swearing now," I said.

"You'm enough to make a saint swear!"

"That's a nice thing to say, ain't it?" I skidded the chair

23

right across the room, with a great row, out of her reach.

"Look at him, wreckin' the furniture!"

I sent a quick glance to the chair, to check that it hadn't really been damaged, then boasted, "I'll sell it for firewood."

Vicky raised her head very sour. "Graeme, why don't you grow up?"

"It was all peaceful till you come up," Babs said.

Now, Babs is a very pretty, sort of plump little bit, with lots of green eye-shadow, and only seventeen, so I was willing to swop to her, instead of trying to answer Vicky, who would be sure to show me up in front of all the other girls. I showed her me fist. "You want a punchin' an' all?"

She giggled. "You wouldn't dare."

"*Wouldn't* I?"

"No, you wouldn't."

So I went for her, and she ran around the table, and I ran the other way, and then we were sort of threatening to run either way, me causing as much trouble as I could by rocking the chairs the others were sitting on.

"Graeme!" Vicky said. "For God's sake – act your age!"

I even woke Jen, who'd got her nose stuck in some woman's magazine in the corner. "He can make more noise – " she said.

"Noise? What noise? I ain't makin' no noise!" I said.

"Oh Graeme – !"

The door opened and the Gaffer came in, sniffing for his dinner. Vicky swung round in her chair and said, "Gaffer, will you tell him?"

The Gaffer looked at his watch. "It's one o'clock," he said, "and you should all be downstairs. What's he been doin'?"

They reeled off my sins.

"Throwing the chairs about."

"Runnin' round, and round like a mad thing."

"Makin' hisself a nuisance . . ."

"Kept pullin' at the chairs."

"Swearin' – sayin' he's going to beat us up."

24

"It sounds like him," the Gaffer said. "Come on all of you, downstairs. Let me have me dinner in peace." They all trooped past us, overalls swishing and heels clipping. I tried to leave too, but the Gaffer stopped me with one long arm. "I'll give it you, throwin' the chairs about," he said. "I have to account for them chairs when they'm broke. What do you think you're playin' at?"

"Nothin'."

"Did you finish them soap-powders?"

"Yeah."

"Right; then you can go and do them stock-cards. That should keep you out of everybody's hair for the afternoon. But before you go, you can stand that chair up again."

So I ran, and put the chair back on its feet, and then I ran down the corridor from the staff-room.

I fetched the stock cards from the office and went back upstairs to the stock-room to do them. It would probably take me all afternoon. They should have been done Monday, but they hadn't, and they had to be done before next Monday. The Gaffer uses them for the order. What they are is, when a load comes in, you write down how many boxes of, say, custard powder you've received, and any received during the week. Then, the next week, you note down how many are left in stock. Take one number from the other, and you have, approximately, how many boxes sold, and you know how many to order for the next week. It may not sound like a long job, but believe me, it is, especially when you're unloading the skips and stacking the boxes in their places in the stock-room as you go on.

I should never have gone to the park. After being in the sunshine I couldn't settle to working in the stock-room. It was sort of dismal – all them dingy boxes, and the dust, and the light sort of yellow. And the walls painted cream. It looked as if they were trying very hard to be white, but failing. I kept thinking how bright it was outside, and yawning, and looking at me watch, and wishing it was five, and feeling

25

browned-off, and not wanting to do the stock-cards. I thought how much better it'd be to work outside. Even if it did rain. I quite like rain. I don't like gloomy, stuffy buildings.

Park gardening. I really liked that idea. I couldn't think why it hadn't come to me before. Why'd I let myself be steered into this job when I could have said, "I want to be a park-gardener!" I don't suppose Dad would have let me.

But there's me – I've been growing date-stones and orange-pips in cups of dirt since I was six. When I was three I was growing mustard and cress on a piece of old sheet. But I never thought of being a gardener. I suppose it's because you don't expect to enjoy your work.

I suppose if I'd told that careers officer bloke that I liked growing things, he'd have said, "What about bein' a park-gardener then?" But I didn't tell him, even though, at the time, I was trying to get over the murder of me African Violet by me mother. She'd over-watered it. Again. I didn't tell him because – I don't know. Because of the way he was, I suppose. With his little cards and his folders, scribbling away, never looking up. He didn't seem to be the kind of bloke who'd be interested in rosemary in pots on the kitchen window-sill. And I wasn't interested in any of his ideas. They sent me to see him five times and he used to sigh when I went in, because we just talked round in circles until we ground to a halt, never getting anywhere. And then he'd scribble a bit more on one of his bits of card, and say, "Well, go away and think about it, and let me know if you come up with anything." And away I'd go, with no intention of letting him know anything, just thankful to have got him off my back again. So it's partly my fault I'm stuck in this job.

Not that I think Dad would have let me be a park-gardener if a thousand careers officers all begged him to in chorus.

But then, I never knew me luck. Maybe I could talk Dad into considering my changing my job, and then maybe I could consider it coolly. Maybe if I told him how bored I was with this job, and just how much I'd like to work outside, if I could find the words that would reach him and really make him understand. . . .

But then, I knew me Dad. Cautious, the word for him is. He'd never do anything like changing his job, and he wouldn't let me do it either if he could help it.

I deliberately stopped myself thinking about it, and went back to the stock-cards. I plugged away and they slowly got done. I was as bored as I was high. My head began to ache a bit, above one eye. I looked at me watch. Ten to four. I sighed, and went to count the prunes.

At five to five the Gaffer came up. "Gray – ?"

I said, "I'm here," before he could decide that I wasn't and go. I was up on the top shelf, right against the ceiling, between a big box of oven-foil and a bigger box of Christmas puddings. He came down the aisle, looking up. He had a wage-packet and a wage-ticket in his hand. "What you doin' up there, Gray?"

"I was checkin' the stuff up here. Them aerosols along there, and this foil."

"How did you get up?"

"I climbed up. Climbed up the shelves."

He looked at the shelves. They're wide-spaced, packed with stuff, and a bit shaky. "You'll break your neck," he said. "Come down and get your money."

I threw the stock-card down and turned around, slithering over the edge of the shelf until me feet touched the next shelf, then edging along and jumping across the aisle to the top of the stack of oxtail soup, and climbing down via (as they say) the minestrone, cream of chicken and Spring Veg.

"I think you've got a bit of mountain goat in you, ain't you? Got a pen?"

"Yeah." I leaned on a nearby box and signed the wage-ticket. Ten pound sixty-nine it said on the packet. It was sealed. "Time to go, is it?" I looked at my watch. "Yeah, five o'clock."

27

The Gaffer's hand thudded on to my shoulder. "Hang about. It is precisely 4.59 and fifty-eight seconds."

"Oh Gaffer – "

"Fifty-eight, fifty-seven, fifty-six, fifty-five, fifty-four, fifty-four, fifty-four – "

"Gaffer – "

He said, "Can you look me straight in the eye and say that you've worked – worked – from half-eight this morning till now?"

I looked him straight in the eye and said, "I have worked from half-eight till now."

"You liar," he said. "What about tea-breaks?"

"Oh Gaffer – "

"What about dinner, and the time you spend talkin' and starin' into space, eh?"

"Oh Gaffer – you can't work – you can't keep your nose on the grindstone for – for every second you'm at work!"

"Why not?" he said, and that mad gleam came into his eye. He tightened his grip on my shoulder and glared into my face. "Why not, eh? There was a damn sight more work done in the days afore they had tea-breaks and dinner-breaks, and allowed talking on the shop-floor!" And he was only half joking. "Tea-breaks!" he said. Tea-breaks are a very sore point with all Gaffers.

"It's five now, Gaffer," I said, hopefully.

"What's your hurry? I thought you enjoyed your work?"

I was tired of the joke. "Well, I don't."

"What?"

"I'm fed up tonight, I want to get out, I ain't done the fire-lighters nor the matches, you do 'em?"

I stood watching him, my weight on one foot, waiting for the second I could leave without offending him too much. He nodded slowly, not very pleased. "Yeah; I suppose I can find the time to do 'em."

"Can I go now?"

"I thought you liked the job. I thought you was happy

28

here, Gray.''

Oh God, now we were going to have the deep, searching questions. What do you want from life? You must realise that in this life. . . . I was itching to get away. I rubbed one foot up and down. ''I am,'' I said. Anything to shut him up. ''I am,'' I said, ''happy – but I'm fed up.''

''Ah – go on, it's five,'' he said. ''Get out me sight.''

So I went, didn't I. I went to the staff-room and fetched me jacket. I ran downstairs, and out through the check-outs. Outside I went up the road, past the church to the bus stop. It had got colder and the day was nearly gone. I got to the bus stop at quarter-past five, at twenty-past it started to rain. At nearly five to six, the Midland Red thoughtfully sent a bus along. I climbed aboard, went halfway up the bus for a seat and was almost thrown off my feet when the driver started off. I collapsed thankfully into a seat, amongst the smell of wet raincoats and rising damp. ''Ten,'' I said to the conductor.

I sank into a coma until my stop and then baled out on to the pink and cream paving-stones outside the estate shops. There were seven shops: a launderette, a chip-shop, a post-office, greengrocery, butcher's, grocer's and one selling baby-clothes, all sheltering from the rain under blue and white blinds. On all other sides were the flats. Everywhere you looked, because you couldn't see their tops without tipping your head right back, and they went side by side, and behind each other, overlapping. But at least they were built on lawns. I ran across the grass, between the flats, and across the road; into the play-ground, along the top of the concrete tube, over the railings and in through the side door of Ward House.

The lift was working. It's cushier than the one at work, less bare, makes less noise and it has a light in it too. Up I went to the fifteenth floor, feeling like the pith in a plant stem – layers of brick and steel all round me. The corridor outside the lift was painted pale yellow, but it was the same as work: windowless, stale, closed-in. I opened the door of our flat with me key and went in.

We've got an L-shaped hall. The door of my bedroom is at the corner of the 'L', then, on the straight, is the living-room and my parents' bedroom, and opposite, the bathroom, and then, at the end, the kitchen. It's all a miracle of miniaturisation. As they say. Like me.

I went into the living-room, and threw me jacket on the settee. I think our living-room's a bit bare. There's the table, with its clean checked cloth, to one side of the balcony windows; there's the telly on its table in the corner by the windows. In front of it is Dad's armchair, with his footstool. Then the settee slants across the room from the corner of the table towards the armchair. By the door as you go in from the hall is a little table with glass ornaments and a vase on it. There's a mirror hanging on the wall behind Dad's chair, away from the fire, because Mother says it's dangerous to have a mirror above a fire. All mounted on a fluffless carpet. I think my jacket on the settee improves it. Mom doesn't.

"Hang your coat up, Graeme."

"I will, in a bit."

"An' will you fetch that washin' in for me?"

I opened the french windows and went out on to the balcony. The windows are always kept closed, because me Mom's terrified that if they're left open we'll all fall out through 'em. She won't go on to the balcony at all if she can help it. It is a bit of a shock. In the flat you could be on the ground, then you step through the windows and wheee! hundred and five feet up in the air!

I brought the washing in and threw it on to the settee. I shut the windows after me again. Mother came in from the kitchen, with her apron on, as always. I get a shock when I see her without her apron. She gave me a fruit cake in a paper-case that was still warm from the oven. "You fetched the washin' in? – Thanks love. There's tea in the pot if you want it and I'll fetch your dinner in a minute. Got your wages?"

I took the packet out and gave it to her. "Thanks," she said, and slipped it into the frilly pocket of her checked pinny. I reckon she looks and smells just how a mother ought to, but I suppose I'm biased there. But, I mean, mothers *ought* to have pinnies, and glasses, and brown curly hair, plump figures and a smell of washing-powder mixed with fruit cake.

"What am the cakes like?" she asked, as she brought my dinner in.

"Smashin'," I said, through a full mouth. I poured myself a cup of tea. She put me dinner on the table and uncovered it. I lifted the cloth and got myself a knife and fork from the drawer in the table. "Don't touch the plate because it's red hot," she said. I sat in. Pork chop, mash, peas and thick gravy. My mouth started to water and I got started.

"Is it nice?" she said.

"Um."

"Had a good day?"

"All right. Pour us another cup of tea?"

"Ar. I could do with one meself . . . Goin' out tonight?"

I splodged me potatoes into me gravy, and stirred me peas about. "No, not tonight. I was goin' to do me lesson – Mom?"

"What?"

"Do you think I could have some more money – or some out the bank?" I filled my mouth quickly, watching her from the corners of my eyes.

"That depends what you want it for, don't it?" She stood, arms folded, waiting for me to speak.

"A shirt," I said.

"A shirt? What do you want a shirt for?"

"I want one for best. One for going out in."

She tutted. "Graeme – you've got one for best." She poured tea. "One for best and two for work. You don't need any more."

I picked up my chop and bit at it. "But – " I said, chewing. "But that one – I don't like it. Gran bought me that one. White. Nobody wears white shirts any more – and them for work I've had since I was ten!"

"Oh, Graeme, don't exaggerate. And there's nothing wrong with a nice white shirt. You look lovely in it."

I sighed. The shirt business was the thin end of the wedge really. I was starting with that. I was fed up with trousers that barely reach me ankle-bone and school pullovers. I said, "Could I have a jacket then – one of them denim jackets, them short uns. I'd pay for it – " I watched her face, but it wasn't very hopeful.

"You've got no need for one. What you want a jacket for? You've got your donkey-jacket."

"What about in the summer though?" I said.

"Then you go to work in your jumper."

I kicked the table leg. "Only kids wear jumpers like them. I could wear one of them denim jackets instead of a jumper."

"They cost too much," she said flatly, stirring her tea.

"*I'd* pay for it."

"You know your father wants you to save the money."

"It's *my* money."

"Graeme – you're not going to waste your money on things you don't need, and that's flat. You know your father wouldn't like it. It's for your own good – we *could* let you spend your money on everything that took your eye, and then when you really want the money, you won't have it. You might want a car, or one day you're going to want to buy a house, maybe, and then you'll be glad you saved. Anyway – anybody'd think you were a girl, worrying so much about clothes." She must have seen I was hurt, because she added, "I'll see about a jacket for your birthday."

"That's not till November!"

"Soon enough – oh, there's your father. Now you shut up about jackets and shirts or there'll be hell to pay." She darted off to the kitchen to get his dinner, and I heard him follow her, so that they could have a quick snog without me watching them. They came in together, well, almost. Dad led, with Mother following ten paces behind, carrying his dinner. Dad squeezed the back of my neck hard. "How's the bread-winner?"

"All right," I said, a bit sour, thinking of jackets and gardening.

"Good, that's all we can hope for." He sat into his dinner, knee to knee with me at the little table, then suddenly took hold of my nose between two fingers and twisted it. I grinned, and a grin sort of grew out of his face – it looked too tough to smile really. He's a little bloke, me Dad, it must run in the family. Little and stocky, what they call 'stiff' round here. He's got maulers of hands, with big knuckles and veins, and his arms am as thick as the table-legs, twice as solid as mine. He's the foreman, the Gaffer, at a little foundry. He knows the job back to front and inside out. He was all grimy and sooty and sandy, and he was starting on the tea already. He can drink three pots of tea straight off. I mean three whole pots, just by himself. That's because it's hot in the foundry and he sweats a lot. You have to be strong to do a job like me Dad's, and he is. He wears this big belt, leather, about two inches wide, and a quarter inch thick, with a big brass buckle, all around his belly. He's broad – brod, we say. That belt goes twice round me and more. I think more to that belt, and the black working shirt, and the foundry boots, than I do to me long, baggy white overall.

I finished before him.

"Go and make another pot of tea, flower."

So I took the pot into the kitchen, put the kettle on the stove and jumped up to sit on the draining board while it boiled. I could have worked in a foundry – got arms like me Dad – with a tattoo, maybe, of a dagger and a snake, like one of the painters that comes to our shop – and a big belt. A big belt that *fitted* me. Taller too; I wouldn't mind being about six foot three like John Wayne, instead of a debatable, and

33

skinny, five foot three.

I used to go down to the foundry with Dad sometimes, Saturdays and school holidays. It's a thing to see. The moulds am made out of sand mixed with resin or something, and they have what they call a pattern to make the mould. They fill a steel box with sand, and they press the pattern down into it. The patterns are usually made of glass-fibre. Then they build more sand over the top of the pattern, and they bake it hard. When that's done, they can lift the sand-mould off the pattern – by hand if it's small enough, but sometimes they have to use a crane. Then the top of the sand-mould's pegged down to the bottom half with tubes to pour the metal through. If the mould's been damaged, these blokes come with tiny little trowels to repair it. It's great to watch 'em, but they won't let you touch, not likely.

They let the iron out of the furnace then – it runs like water and lights the place up. They run it into a crucible, and carry it across and pour it through the tubes into the mould. Me Dad has to know just where these tubes should be, or there are places the metal don't reach because of air-pockets, and the casting's ruined. And sometimes the tubes will look full, when the mould's not half-full. It's really sort of exciting, watching 'em cast something like that. 'Course, this is the old-fashioned way. In a big foundry, it'd be all mechanised. Dad's place is only a small shop. It's red-hot inside, and dark, and the black sand gets everywhere. The only light's from the furnace and the molten metal, and the bit that comes through the door. The blokes wear long aprons, and clogs with leather flaps to stop the metal getting into their shoes. Dad used to make me put an apron and flaps on before I could watch 'em. They sweat so much they drink like fish after. They've got throats like drains.

I slid off the draining-board when the kettle boiled, poured the boiling water on the tea and stirred it. I took it in and Dad poured himself a cup right off.

"Here you are," Mom said. She took my wage packet from

her pocket and dropped it on the table.

"What's this?" Dad said. "Money for me?"

"M'wages," I said, trying not to grin, but grinning anyway.

"Wages? You – wages?" Then the Dawn of Realisation bit, the wink and nose-tap to Mom. "Oh. I *forgot*. He's a *worker* now." The business became serious. "Ten sixty one. Right, that's three fifty to your mother, leaves – "

"Seven eleven," I said.

We waited while he caught up with my arithmetic. "Ar. Seven eleven. Now what's two into seven eleven?"

We do it every week, but he never remembers. I do. "Three pound fifty-five and half-pence," I said.

"Right." He took out his wallet and gave me three pound notes, and then the fifty-five and half-pence from his pocket. He gave my mother a fiver and said, "Keep the change," and then put my wage packet, unopened, into his wallet, reminding himself, "Got to put three fifty-five and half into Graeme's account." He got up from the table and stroked my head like I was a cat. "Don't seem two minutes ago since he was walking under the table without bumpin' his head – and now he's bringin' home a wage." He sat in his armchair. "Bring us another cup of tea, flower."

"And me," Mom said.

I poured three cups of tea, while I ran through my own arithmetic. Net amount: three fifty-five and half. Bus fares for a week: one twenty. Leaves: two pound thirty-five and half. Weekly allowance for dinners: one pound. Leaves one pound thirty-five and half. Tea money: fifteen pence. Leaves one pound twenty and half pence.

One pound twenty and half pence.

Visit to the pictures: fifty-five pence. Single record: fifty-five pence. A night out and I could spend me whole allowance. Or more and finish up wàlking home and to work – ain't it a shame, eh? But it's a tight budget.

I gave out the tea and, drinking mine, wandered into me

bedroom to have a look at me cactus. It hadn't opened yet, but it was threatening to. There was a frill of bright pink petals showing from the bud. Cerise, me mother calls it, like her best hat. Her best hat!

I crouched down by the cactus and stroked the frill of petals. "Hello," I said. "Not open yet? Come on, open, hurry up and open. I want to see you open." I've got this bottle of liquid fertiliser on me dressing-table – or I did have. Couldn't find it.

Then I saw that me room had been tidied, tie put away, curtains changed from yellow-check to green-check. So I looked for the fertiliser in the drawers of the dressing-table. Mother had put it in there, along with me Dudley Bug – a fossil of a kind of prehistoric insect – and my gurkha-type sheath-type an uncle had given me, and my Mexican jumping-beans in their plastic tube, a present from the same uncle. I took them all out again and put them on top of the dressing-table, along with the Chinese, Australian and African coins, the big gold watch that had been given me Grandad Thorpe, the plastic shrunken head and the big brass' 'penny', the memorial plaque, with Britannia and 'Samuel Bowen, He died for Freedom and Honour' on it; and the gun-button from a Spitfire's joy-stick out of the other drawer. I poured a drop of fertiliser on to the cactus, and screwed the bottle shut again.

I picked up the jumping-beans and tucked the tube into my hands. You get 'em warm, see, and they start to hop about. I pulled the box of marigold seedlings out from under the bed. They were planted in one of the boxes the grapes come in at work, and stood on one of the big polythene bags the toilet rolls come in. They were growing very well, I'd move 'em out on to the balcony. Mom wouldn't mind one box. I'd have to start collecting empty margarine tubs and cress pots from work, foil trays from frozen pies, that kind of thing, to plant 'em out in. I fetched a jugful of water from the kitchen – watered the Busy Lizzie while I was on – and watered my date-palm, vine and lemon-plant. I took the marigolds and the plastic sheet from under the bed and carried them out on to the balcony, watered them there.

"You haven't spilt dirt on the floor, have you?" Mother said.

"I kept the plastic under it."

"Leave him be," Dad said. "He won't hurt."

Back in my room, I reached under the bed for my lesson. The pile of pinup magazines had been gathered into a neat pile and put where I could reach them easily when I was lying in bed. Now how's that? What did she do that for? There's some of them mags old C give me, and I shouldn't think Mother would approve of 'em. Perhaps she hadn't looked at 'em. I took the lesson and went back into the living-room. The jumping beans hadn't moved at all. I thought they must be dead, but put 'em against the tea-pot anyway.

I took my books and the lesson and sat down in my usual place, on the floor, leaning my back against the arm of Dad's chair. Mother had put her feet up on the settee. Dad began to scratch the top of my head with one finger until it felt as if bees were buzzing in my skull. "Gerroff," I said. He laughed and pulled a single hair out of my head. Ouch. I rubbed at the sore place. Dad sniggered and twisted my ear. "Oh, blummin' hell, Dad, lay off!"

"Go an' make us another pot of tea then."

So I got up and went, didn't I.

2

The next day was Saturday. I like Saturdays because I get a chance to give orders instead of taking them. Bancroft's employs four Saturday workers, see, schoolkids, two chaps and two wenches. The chaps are Ian and Mike; the wenches Eileen and Kate. I can tell them what to do. I try to give 'em the impression that I'm in charge really, and the only reason I'm not openly the manager is that Bancroft's don't want to break the poor old Gaffer's heart by telling him he's past it.

I came downstairs, buttoning my overall up, and found that the bread had arrived at the loading-door. I pushed open one of the swing doors into the shop and saw Mike standing there, stunned with having to get up on a Saturday morning. He's fourteen, this Mike is, two years younger than me, and my head comes about level with his middle overall button. He starts at these big, skin-head-type boots, and goes up, then up some more, then bends over, then straightens out, and then carries on up. His neck slopes forward out of his shoulders about a foot, with his head on the end. Must be about six foot two. He could play the beanstalk to my Jack. He makes me want to spit, I mean, you can tell, can't you? I said, "Mike – get in here. You got to help me get the bread in."

He sloped towards me. When he walks he leans so far forward from his boots he'd fall over if they hadn't such a grip on the ground. He wasn't pleased. I'm not very popular with the Saturday lads. I leaned against the door to keep it open while he went through, passing me. "You take some trays round," I said, and went to fetch the trolley from the cooked meats counter. Mrs. Harris was smiling on the fruit counter. "I can hear you giving your orders," she said. "Don't think I can't." I grinned and went on, round the biscuit shelf.

I met Ian coming in. Ian's not as tall as Mike. Must be all of half an inch shorter. I stand almost as high as his lapels. What have they been putting in the orange juice since I stopped getting it free? Why is every snotty-nosed little ten-year-old bigger than me just lately? And you ought to see Vicky smile at Ian, even though he is five years younger than she is, and she goes running to him to move boxes for her, and says goodbye to him. Her never asks *me* to move boxes for her. "You'm late," I said.

"I know," he said, and grinned.

"You'd better step on it then, hadn't you?"

He just grinned and walked on past.

I fetched the trolley and took it into the back, where I loaded it up with trays of bread: wrapped, sliced, batch, brown, wholemeal, cobs, crusty, milk, scones, sugar-buns – the lot. I was surrounded by a sort of warm, cloudy, fluffy bread-smell. It always smells great by the bread-fixture.

While I was loading the bread, I could look across into the park through the open loading-door. There was Bancroft's yard, all concrete and rubbish, and the road, and the houses and office-blocks; and dropped in the middle, this park that the sun seemed to be shining on specially, so the daffodils glowed all hazy, and you could see the bark-dust under the trees, and the grass, and the fountain making a cool, splattery ring round itself. I slammed a tray of bread on top of two others on the trolley and sighed. "I wish I was out there instead of shut up in here," I said to Mike.

He turned his head and looked out at the park. The side of his face. Blank. He didn't know what I was talking about. He dismissed it. "I'll take these cobs in."

"Don't be daft!" I said, for no other reason than to be awkward. "It's that sliced bread you want to take in. Don't you know enough to find your best seller yet? You get the best seller on the shelves first."

He said nothing, but was very slow and deliberate about putting down the cobs and picking up the sliced bread. I went to the office and got the bread-order. The Gaffer always writes down how many of which kinds we've got to keep, and hangs it from one of the hooks on his office-shelves by a bull-dog clip. I took it down to the loading-door, and began to read it. Mike came back. "I want them," I said, taking the wire bread-trays off him. "You take that lot in." I nodded to the trolley.

"Yes, sergeant-major," he said.

"Very funny. Hurry up."

Fourteen sliced, eighteen crusty, ten batch, six Welsh, three milk – I found them and fitted them into the tray as neatly as their shapes would allow. I went to help Mike unload the bread on to the fixture, and afterwards to pile the bread-trays outside the loading-door. If I left it to him, he'd just throw 'em down so they'd all fall over when anybody passed by 'em. As we loaded the trolley again, I pointed to the tray I'd filled with bread, and said, "Don't touch that, that's the order."

"I *know*," he said.

"Just to be sure," I told him.

"You don't have to keep telling me. I've been working here months now. I know."

"All right, all right," I said, feeling I was getting the worst of it. "Let's get on."

I shoved the trolley into the shop. It's very difficult to steer, that trolley. Goes everywhere but where you want it to go. But I managed to get it round to the fixture without running down more than one old age pensioner. He was very nice about it. Threatened to get me sacked. And so to the fixture and the unloading. Load it up, unload it. Ho, hum. I yawned. Already the air in the shop was stale. Breathing was like being injected with boredom. I mean, being bored wasn't something you became in that place; it was that place.

As we shoved bread into rows on the fixture, I said to Mike, "Wouldn't you like to work outside?"

"What?" he said. "Have we got to sweep the yard then?"

Oh Christ. "No," I said. "I mean, wouldn't you like to be – well, to be – a park-gardener, like?"

"A park-gardener?"

"Yeah! Don't you know what one of them is? They plant out all them floral clocks and that you get in parks, you know. They do a lot of gardenin', they'm noted for it."

He carried on with the bread, shoving it on to the top shelf with no stretching at all. "I wouldn't work outside," he said, when I thought he wasn't going to answer. "What about when it rains and in the winter? Not me."

I leaned against the fixture and looked at him – looked up at him – while he finished the tray of bread. He had this posh voice and he came from Oakham. That wouldn't mean anything to you, but to me, and people round here, it means big fancy houses, detached, and all different from the one next door, with trees in the street, scroll-work gates, big lawns and two cars. "What are you goin' to do then? Suppose you'll work in office, won't you?"

He looked down at me, from his great height like, and said, "I'm going to be a doctor."

"Oh, are yer?" I clanged wire-trays on to the trolley and wheeled it away. "Well, come on, ruddy Dr. Kildare." I rattled the trolley away around the aisles into the back, to collect more bread. "What you work here for then?" I said. "You live in one of them big houses along Oakham, don't you?"

His mouth was tight as he put a tray of rolls on the trolley. He knew I wasn't just being curious. He knew I was trying to

41

rile him. I bloody was too.

"Yeah," he said.

"Which one?"

"Number thirty-eight."

"Which one's that?"

He didn't want to answer, but I was waiting on him. "It's got green shutters," he said in the end.

"Blimey! Not that big white one with the chestnut tree and the half mile of garden? The one called 'Reg-Vi'?" I grinned all over my chops as his face turned a deep blood colour.

"I suppose so," he said through gritted teeth. "It's not all that big."

"It's a damn sight bigger than our flat. Got a greenhouse an' all. Hey, it's a bloody landmark, that house of yours. Like a pub. 'Turn left at the Huntsman, then go along to that big white house with the green shutters.' If you live there and you're goin' to be a doctor, how come you've got to work here Saturdays and Friday nights?"

He leaned on the trolley and said, "I'm not hurting you by working here, am I?"

"I just wondered, that's all, Doctor."

"You're a bloody mixer, you are."

"Language, Doctor, language."

"Language yourself."

"Why'd you have to work here though?" I insisted. "Don't you get pocket money? I used to. Me Dad used to give me fifty pence every week. When I was fourteen. I only got twenty-five before then." He didn't answer. I said, "I'd have thought your Mom and Dad, bein' so well off, would have give you pocket money. Do they reckon havin' a greenhouse makes up for it then?"

"I get pocket money," he said. "But I don't reckon it's fair for Mom and Dad to pay for everything, so I got a job and I just happened to get a job here – sergeant-major."

"All right, Doctor. How much d'you get then? Pocket

money I mean, I know how much you get here – two pound fifty – how much d'your Mom and Dad give you?"

"Four pound," he said.

"Come off it," I said.

"I've got nothing to come off," he said, all airy.

"Oh come on – you can tell a good tale, now sing us a song."

"Look – don't believe me if you like but it makes no difference. You asked, I told you. I get four pound from my Dad. Six pound fifty with what I earn here." He took the last three trays of bread into the shop.

Good, ain't it? Three pound fifty-five and half pence I'm allowed from me own wages. He gets four pound give to him for doing nothing. I think I'll turn Communist. I caught up with him at the bread-fixture. "I'd like to work outside."

"Would you?" he said.

"Yeah, I would, Doctor Kildare."

"Well, why don't you then?"

"I'm thinking about it, Doctor Kildare. I'm going to give in my notice and then I'll go round to the Labour and get me an outdoor job. That's what I'm going to do." I added, "You got to help me with the baling and tidying the back up after."

I took the trolley back to the cooked meats and we were walking to the back, when the Gaffer passed us. He suddenly turned round and pointed at me, so that I nearly walked into his finger and impaled meself. I stood, fixed by the pointing finger and staring eyes, wondering what the hell I'd done wrong now.

"Profits and percentages," the Gaffer said.

I grinned with relief. "Oh yeah. I got it upstairs, that lesson."

"Good." The Gaffer fell in with us. "You can go and fetch it and bring it up to the office."

"Right," I said.

"You'll need to know profit and percentages – you've got the exam in about two months' time, haven't you?"

Mike said, "I thought you was giving notice, Gray?"

The Gaffer looked down at me. "Gray – ?"

"I'll just go and fetch that lesson," I said quickly, ran into the back, and belted up the stair. It was funny, I had to admit that, and I bet Mike thought it was a good laugh too, but he'd dropped me in it.

I was slow going up the office steps. When I opened the door, the Gaffer was sorting through papers. I shut the door and sat down on the other stool with one leg under me. I curled the other leg round the stem of the stool and leaned over the desk. It was the time-sheets the Gaffer was doing. He scribbled away, then shuffled 'em together, and knocked 'em square. "What's this about you giving notice?"

"Nothin', Gaffer."

"Don't you like it here?"

I writhed. " 'S nothin' – I just said I'd like to work outside, that's all."

"So you're leavin', are you?"

He was plaguing me. I started to get red. Served me right, I suppose, for plaguing Mike. It was all coming back to me. "No – I was just – "

"Oh well, let's have a look at these profits and percentages." He took the lesson from me, opened it at the example, where my book was folded in it. Then he said, "I *knowed* there was something I was going to tell you. After you'd left last night there was a bloke in here after you. A real hippy he was."

"Hippy?" I said, surprised.

"Yeah. Long hair – jeans – real hippy. 'Graeme Bowen work here?' he says. I says, 'Ar, but he's gone home.' 'Saft sod,' this bloke says and walks off. 'Saft sod,' he says and walks off."

Things were clicking and joining in my head. Two and two fitted neatly together. "Was he a tall feller, well, pretty tall," I said. "Fairish hair?"

"I didn't look at him that good," the Gaffer said, paying more attention to my lesson than to me.

44

"I bet it was Derek," I said.

"Hmm? Derek? Who's he when he's at home?"

"Me brother Derek."

"Your brother – oh, yes. It *was* you said your brother had left home, wasn't it?"

"Yeah, that's right."

The Gaffer was interested again. "Well, he looked a hippy."

"He ain't hippy – " Matter of fact, he could have been anything. I hadn't seen him for about eight years. He left home when I was eight, so it would be eight years. He'd be – twenty-five or thereabouts. I couldn't picture him as a hippy, or as twenty-five. I could only remember my big brother, the one who'd sat on me bed until I'd gone to sleep, when I was six and scared of the dark.

The Gaffer finished reading the example and said, "What don't you understand?"

"Well – everythin'. I can't get 'em to work out."

"Ah – " And so began the big battle. He explained, and I concentrated, and at the end I still didn't understand. So he'd start again, and I'd get a glimmering, and then the glimmering would be swamped by more explanations. And then I'd get it, and work out a profit for him, and half-way through I'd get lost, and sit back, and he'd sigh and finish the sum. By eleven o'clock I had this thin fragile thread of understanding running through all the confusion and mistakes.

"Got it now?"

"Yeah," I said scowling, "I think so."

"You'd better. The exams am comin' up, remember. Two months ain't long. Go on, get out me sight. But if there's anythin' you don't understand – you know, I'm always willin' to try and explain it."

"Right – er – thanks, Gaffer." I went down the office steps.

"Gray," he called after me. "You may as well go up for your break now. Tell Winnie to make me a bacon sandwich."

45

"Right, Gaffer." I stood at the bottom of the steps, my hand on the rail. "You want tomato sauce on it?"

"No."

"I'll tell her."

I was hungry myself. I fancied something to eat, but, like me Mom says, can't eat good plain food. Got to have something fancy. I went and fetched one of these individual apple-pies off the cake-fixture, they're four pence. I paid for it down at the check-outs and ran on into the back and up the stairs. But at the top I slowed down and trudged along the corridor into the staff-room. The daylight blazed in through the windows and made me feel grubby and tired after the gloom in the rest of the shop.

"Hello, chick," Winnie said. "I thought you must have had your break stopped." The Gaffer does stop your break sometimes.

"No," I said, but it was too much trouble to explain. I threw the lesson on the table. "The Gaffer's coming up. He wants a bacon sandwich."

She looked flustered, and banged the cups on the draining-board about a bit. "I'll put the kettle on, love. Does he want sauce?"

"No." I sat down at the table, and leaned my head in my hands. I closed my eyes to shut out the light. It only made me want to be outside and I couldn't leave until one o'clock. And I thought of them exams coming up and felt ill.

"You all right, love? Got headache, have you?"

"Wha'? Oh – no. No, I was just thinkin' of that exam I've got to take. An' then – " Smashin' day outside.

If I was to pack this job in, I'd miss the exam as well as getting to work in a park. I mean, whenever I think of that exam, which is as seldom as possible, believe me, I can feel it like a ten-ton weight quivering over my head on a cotton thread. And if I fail that exam, it's going to drop on me. There's not Dad or the Gaffer going to be pleased. I mean, I know the stuff, exceptin' the profits and percentages, but I'm not very

46

good at writing it all out so that other people can understand what I'm on about, and the Gaffer says me handwriting looks like I used a pig's trotter dipped in tar.

I'd really like to pack it all in and work outside with plants. I would.

To start with, I'd have to get round Dad. I don't know if Dad could stop me changing jobs, by law like, but he could certainly make me wish I'd never been born if I get across him. Just by shouting he could do that. He's only ever hit me once that I can remember. I was cheeking me mother and he clouted the side of me head. Nearly knocked me off me feet. I was dizzy, I can tell you. I've never lipped Mother while he was around since.

I know one thing. If I talk to him about changing me job, he won't listen to me. I've always found that the best way to get round me Dad is to talk Mom into getting round him for me. Not that she can always handle him, and sometimes he gets mad with her. Makes me feel guilty, that.

Winnie put a cup of tea in front of me. "Oh – thanks, Win." I stirred it slowly. I'd have a word with Mom when I got back. If she was going to tackle Dad she deserved a re-ward, though –

The Gaffer came in, and sat down. Winnie put tea and a bacon sandwich in front of him. I drank tea, the spoon wobbling round in front of my face.

"Why your brother leave home then, Gray?"

"Eh?"

"Your brother – why'd he leave home?"

It took me a minute or two to think. I'd been only eight. "He didn't get on with me Dad. He went to lodge with these friends he had."

"Just walked out like that?" The Gaffer was really inter-ested. He thought he'd got on to the trail of a genu-ine dropout hippy, as featured in the *News Of the World*.

"He used to come back to start with," I said. "But there was always fights and arguments. So he just stopped comin'.

47

Haven't seen him since."

"Don't you ever go to see him?"

"Don't know where he lives. Just somewhere in Oldbury. And he might not live there any more."

"Oh that is terrible," Winnie said. She whined, "I couldn't let my sons just leave like that."

"I don't think I could," the Gaffer said. "How old was he when he went, Gray?"

"Er – " I did some arithmetic. "Seventeen."

"Seventeen." The Gaffer shook his head. "If it had been me, I should have to have fetched him back."

I didn't know whether Dad had tried to get Derek to come back or not. It sounded to me like one of those things that are easier said than done. I could remember them always arguing – Decker coming in late and Dad hitting the ceiling, or Decker coming in drunk and Dad hitting the ceiling, and both of 'em playing Hamlet, yelling and shouting and cussing one another, and getting down to throwing punches and bottles, and Decker threw a full, hot tea-pot at Dad once, he got so wicked. And Mom standing there, saying, "You shouldn't do this in front of the kid," meaning me. But I can't remember much else, and Mom and Dad never talk about it. They don't make a big dark secret out of it, they've just put it out of their minds like.

The Gaffer sent me downstairs when I'd had a second cup of tea. "There's not a lot to do," he said. "Mike and Ian have done the baling and the back, but tell you what – the pickles was nearly emptied last night. Get one of the Saturday lads and fill it up."

So I went downstairs and found Mike, but he was helping old Claz on the fruit, so I had to fetch Ian. He was talking to Vicky on the check-outs, while pretending to be moving the empty baskets the customers had left out of the way. He was leaning on the top of the till, on the stamp-dispenser, and saying something about 'A' levels. I suppose he's going to be another bloody doctor.

"You've got to come and help me with the sauces," I said, "and do summat for your wages."

"Oh God, look what's come," Vicky said.

Ian smiled down at me. "O.K." He really gets up my nose, worse than Mike. At least Mike's skinny, if he is tall. Ian isn't.

He followed me, grinning, to the pickles and I couldn't think of anything to say that would show him I was in charge. We made a list of all the pickles and sauces that were needed, and went up to the stock-room to fetch them on a skip. We shoved the skip round to the pickles-fixture, and I went to fetch the price-book from the office.

I come back past the biscuit-fixture, where Eileen and Kate were packing in. Kate's a skinny little bird, with short cut hair, long pointed nose, scruffy jeans . . . Eileen don't look real. Looks as if she's made of sugar. She's small, shorter than me, and round, nicely rounded. She's got a tiny little pointed face with great brown eyes and rosy red cheeks. And her hair's black and shiny, hanging all down her back, past her waist. Claz can't keep his hands off it. He's always lifting it up off her neck, or combing it with his fingers.

Anyway, these two watched me all across the shop. Kate saw me come through the double doors with the price-book and whispered something to Eileen. Then they watched me come past the fridge – I stared back, trying to make them look away. When I came level, they were still watching me. I stopped. "What's up?" I said. "Never seen a handsome, debonair man-of-the-world before?"

"No, I never have. I still haven't," Kate said.

"That's nice," I said. "That's nice, that is."

"Biscuits are." Oh, she was a sharp one, no doubt about it.

"I wasn't on about the biscuits – "

"You meant me!" Kate said, giggling. "Oh thanks, sorry I can't say the same about you!"

I looked around, did a double-take, as if lost for words,

49

then marched down the biscuit aisle. "I'll punch your ear-'ole."

Kate dodged behind Eileen, who had stood stiff and shy all through our routine. I tried to catch her, but she dodged the other way. I was left face to face with Eileen. "I'll give her a one-er when I catch hold of her," I told 'Leen. "And you an' all! What was that you was shoutin'?"

The rest of her face turned as rosy pink as her cheeks, and she looked down at her feet. So I left her alone, and kicked some biscuits along the deck, so that I could get round to Kate, who skipped away down the aisle.

Now this was something different from Vicky, who always stood and outfaced me when I tried to start something like this with her. I took off in full pursuit of Kate, tally-ho and yoicks, when I heard my master's voice. "What's all this here?" The Gaffer was leaning on the dairy-fridge, watching us.

"It's her fault, Gaffer," I said, pointing ungallantly at Kate.

He nodded. "Ar," he said. "Pickles." So I went, didn't I.

I spent the rest of the morning pricing and packing in pickles – and running upstairs to give the butcher orders, and showing people where to find things, and adding up shopping bills for old ladies – but mainly pricing and packing pickles. I tried to get at Ian the same way I had Mike, but he said he don't care what he is when he leaves school, and he don't get any pocket money at all. And he grins. Whatever you say, he grins. I gave up trying to rile him after a bit, and we were pretty friendly until I left at one o'clock.

Before I went to catch me bus, I walked down into the main part of the town, to the arcade. There's this shop there that sells these fancy things you don't see anywhere else: white statues with hardly any shape, and doilies, and queer brooches and necklaces. It was Vicky showed me the place, she was always buying herself jewellery from it. I used to go about with her in the dinner-time, see. I'd talk her into

50

letting me buy her a cup of coffee and a cake, and then, when we got to the counter, she'd turn round and say she couldn't take my money off me, because it'd be like taking money off her little brother, and so she'd pay for it herself. I ask you. And once she paid for mine as well and that really made me mad, I felt so daft. But a fat lot of good being mad did me.

Anyway, I peered into the window of this shop. There were these big, heavy necklaces, sort of like dragons, in bright orange and yellow. Right up Vicky's street, but not the sort of thing our Mom'd like at all. And there were a lot of silver lockets, and gold, out of my price range. And big crosses that I couldn't afford either, and ugly lumps of stone on chains. Then I saw these others, hanging down from a shelf. They were made of shells and had a notice tied to them, 'Genuine shells. Limited stock. 70p each.' I went in and bought one. Then I ran up the hill and caught my bus, a different one from usual, which meant I had to walk in from the edge of the estate, past the one or two houses, with gardens. I wish we had one of them, but they've mostly got old people living in them. All the rest of the estate – the Pleck Estate, it is – is flats, the tower blocks, and some with just three storeys. But all flats. I came to Ward House and went up in the lift, let myself into our flat.

"Hello, love," Mom said. I threw my jacket on to the settee. "Graeme, hang your coat up." I gave her the paper bag. "What's this?"

"Don't say I never buy you nothin'," I said, and then dodged embarrassment by going to my bedroom, to have a look at my cactus. It still hadn't really flowered. I had a quick flip through the pin-up magazines and went back into the living-room when I smelt my dinner – rabbit casserole, all stewed and juicy in a big red pot. Mom had put the shell-necklace on, but she didn't mention it, just said, "Help yourself, have what you want and I'll put the rest back on to keep warm for your father."

Dad knocks off at one on a Saturday too, if he's lucky, but

he doesn't come home till a lot later. It's across the road into the pub first, and then he might go back to do some paper-work.

"It's a lovely necklace, Gray. What's it for?" She'd got all strained and embarrassed about asking. That's why I don't really like giving or receiving presents, or asking or getting help. People only come over all embarrassed.

"It ain't for anythin'," I said.

"I'll just wear it today, I think, and then I'll keep it for special occasions."

"Don't you like it then?" I asked.

" 'Course I like it. What you mean?"

"Well, you just said you'd keep it for special occasions. That means you'm goin' to put it in that box in your bed-room, and that's the last we'll see of it."

She looked a bit put out. "I didn't mean that at all, and you know it. I only meant I didn't want it to get spoilt or broke – and it would if I wore it all the time. So I'll keep it for best, for when we go out."

"You never go out," I said. Which was true. The last time I could remember Dad taking her out was when I was about ten, and they dumped me on me Gran Thorpe while they went to the pictures. Mind, it wasn't so bad as I make it sound, because I liked me Gran Thorpe then, and she made flap-jacks, and we watched the telly and had a laugh. But that was me Mom's last outing. Dad won't even take her to the pub, because he reckons pubs ain't the place for women. He says that if Mom was the kind of woman that went into pubs, he never would have married her.

"All right then," Mom said, "all right. I'll wear it on birthdays and high holidays." She poured us both a cup of tea. "Did your Gaffer tell you how to do them sums?"

"Damn, I've left the lesson at work!" I said, but then nodded. "Yeah, he did." I was bothered about how to twist the subject round to park-gardening.

Mom sat down at the table. "I met Mrs. Alton, used to live

52

next door to we down the street. Her daughter's got married, you remember Wendy, her daughter."

"Um," I said. I couldn't see how I was to draw a comparison between Mrs. Alton's daughter's wedding and park gardening.

"Her husband's dead though – Mrs. Alton's husband. Been dead two years."

My hopes rose. "Where've they buried him?" I asked.

This sudden and morbid interest of mine threw her off balance for a second. "Oh – I dunno – didn't think to ask."

"Somebody has to look after cemeteries," I said, trying to lead in.

She frowned, puzzled. "Yes, the Vicar, I suppose. Mrs. Alton was telling me how nice the one married her daughter was. . . ." She prattled away and I decided it was no use trying to be subtle. I waited until her talk died out, probably through my lack of interest. Then I said, "I'd like to be a park-gardener."

"You what?"

"I'd like to be a park-gardener." What is it about park-gardeners that everybody stands round and gawps? I didn't say 'ferret-sexer'. Somebody has to be a park-gardener.

Mother turned snotty. "Oh well – I'd like to be a lot of things. I'd like to be a millionaire, or a filmstar. I'd like to live in a house instead of a flat."

This brought me up short with my mouth open. I remembered that Mom spent nearly all her time in this air-borne rabbit-hutch of ours, scared even to go out on the balcony. She goes out to the shops now and then, and sometimes she meets the woman next door as she's going in or coming out of her flat, and has a chat, but mostly she's on her own until Dad and me get home. I decided that as soon as I'd talked her into softening Dad for me, I'd turn the talk back to Mrs. perishin' Alton, and try to take an interest.

"I want to pack in me job and try to get one as a park-gardener."

53

She stared at me as if I'd run berserk, or beseck, as we say.

"You know I like garden – growing things. You know I do. You're always complaining about the dirt – and I'm fed up with the supermarket."

"Your father won't like it," she said, with satisfaction.

"Ah," I said.

I must take after me mother. All I said was, "Ah" and she was with me straight away. She nodded, her mouth crimped. "And you want me to sound him out and soften him up. I know." She touched the shell necklace. I wish she hadn't done that. Just that little movement made me guilty all over. Not a present, a bribe.

"I'm not sure I'd want you to take an outdoor job – out in all weathers –"

She was only being contrary. "Mom."

She sighed. "He's not going to like it."

"I know."

She looked at me. I gave her a comic smile – quick grin, then solemn again. She smiled back and nodded. "I'll talk to him for you, when I get the chance."

"When?"

"When I get the chance. When he's in a good mood. It'll be no good askin' him today or tomorrow – Monday maybe. I'll make him an apple crumble for his dinner."

I grinned. "Mrs. Alton's husband died, you say?"

"Oh, I don't know," she said, and took the casserole into the kitchen.

Dad came in about four o'clock, and I got up to make him a pot of tea. Really I wanted to get out of his way until he'd decided what mood to be in. But I met him in the doorway of the living-room, which he filled. He was grimy and sooty and sandy, red-faced, merry, drunk as a lord. "You haven't missed 'Doctor Who'," I said, joking, a bit nervous. "I'm just goin' to put the kettle on."

He beamed all over his face at me, and came at me with open arms. I tried to dodge round him, but he boxed me in.

He took hold of my elbows and boosted me up, right up, clasping his arms around under my behind like I was a little kid. My head bumped the ceiling. "Lay off, Dad," I said, ducking, and trying to squirm loose.

"My little lad," he said. Drunk as a tadpole he was. He gets like this. Starts wanting to wrestle and that, which is fine, but he gets carried away. He'd break your arm laughing. Or your neck. I could just see him dropping me to see if I'd bounce. To be honest, I don't much like getting hurt.

"Dick, put him down and stop fooling about, and come and sit down," Mom said sternly. She was worried that he'd give hisself a heart-attack, carting me around like that.

He whirled around the room in circles, still holding me up, going "Wheee!" like a lunatic and making the whole flat shake. Then he dropped me. I was expecting that, luckily. "Big saft Aynoch," I said, staggering backwards to keep my balance.

He pounced on me then, grabbing me round the waist, twisting one arm up behind my back with a crack. I said, "Ow! Lay off, lay – " It would be all right if he was like Phil's father, always wrestling and gaming, but he only games when he's drunk, and then he's proper vicious with it.

He started giving a commentary. "And now the Ward Crusher has got an arm-lock on the Kid, and it looks as if the fight is going to be over very soon, very soon now – " He took me on his hip and tipped my feet off the floor, my head swinging dizzily down. I might have enjoyed it if I had been ten years younger and hadn't got my arm twisted up behind my back. But you expect to be allowed to go on with a bit of dignity when you get to my age. Still, I didn't fight back. It seemed to me that I was going to get dropped on my head soon enough, without bringing it on myself.

Mom came, her skirt swishing round me. "Dick! Put him down, you'm going to hurt him,"

I felt she could have put it more tactfully than that.

"Aah, I won't hurt him. You know I won't hurt him."

"I don't know anythin' of the sort! You don't know your own strength. Now put the kid down and leave him be. Go and sit down and I'll bring you your dinner and some tea."

Dad started to turn around, and the rosy carpet went past my pumping eyes in a blur. All my head was beating, full of blood it must have been. I was getting sick, like on a round-about. "I'm only gamin'," Dad said.

"It might be only a game to you, but you're not the one that gets hurt! Dick! Are you going to put him down? I'll fetch the neighbours in, I swear it!"

Even upside-down I had to smile at the idea of Mom fetching the neighbours in, but it must have worried Dad. Or maybe he was just bored. "Oh for cryin' out loud!" he said, and let me roll on to the floor. My shoulder cracked again and I fell with a thump. Dad flounced off and almost toppled on to the settee, which cranked its springs. "I don't know! Them underneath must wonder what we'm playin' at!" Mom said. "You might have a bit of thought for them if for nobody else!" Dad muttered.

Mom went on, "But then, I suppose you've been in that pub all afternoon. Honestly, you're not fit to live with when you're drunk!"

"I had three pints, three pints!" Dad said. He named the pub opposite the foundry as if that made the beer weaker. "I went in the 'Parrot' and had three pints!"

"Not countin' them he had in the 'Junction', the 'Navvy', the 'Chicks', the 'Struggler', the 'Green Man' and the 'Salamander'," I said, sitting on the floor, rubbing my shoulder.

He reared up over the back of the settee and said, "You keep out of our arguments, young man, else you'll be feeling the back of my hand."

"Don't you start on him just because you've been told a few home truths," Mom said. "It ain't his fault you drink too much – I'll go and fetch your dinner."

"Graeme," Dad said, when she'd gone, "come and switch the telly on for me. It's too much effort to get up."

"You're too drunk, you mean," I said, as I walked wide round the settee to turn the set on.

"Now don't you start, me old son. A few drinks never hurt anybody. Swop it over, 'Doctor Who' ain't on that side." I pressed the button in, and the electronic music and whirling galaxies of 'Doctor Who' roared up. "Come and sit by your poor old Dad, flower, and console him in his age and weakness," Dad said, smoothing the place beside him on the settee. He talks like that when he's drunk.

"I've got to go and help Mom," I said. It's wisest to keep out of his way when he's drunk. He grabbed at me as I went past, but missed by a mile.

I went into the kitchen rubbing me shoulder, which was still sore. "He's a nutter," I said.

"Graeme. You shouldn't say things like that about your father." Every word I say is taken at face value.

"He is though. You can't do this, you can't do that – then a couple of drinks and he's all fun and games. 'Cept he half kills you."

"Now, Graeme. You know he dotes on you. You know he'd do anythin' for you – or me. He ain't like some, violent. He just gets boisterous, and he don't realise that you and me ain't as strong as him."

"Oh it ain't that!" I said quickly. "It's not that I mind. He don't hurt me."

"Then take his dinner in, go on."

So I went, didn't I.

3

Sunday was a bad day, like it usually is in our house. Dad was touchy, spoiling for a fight. Me and Mom couldn't breathe without him jumping down our throats. It all came from a hangover, and lying in bed too long.

I went to see a mate of mine about four o'clock. He lives on the fifth floor of Saltwell House. I thought we might go for a walk somewhere, just killin' time, you know – 'wenching' me Dad would call it. Or he might take me on the pillion of his motor-bike, no harm in hoping. But he never would let me drive it.

But when I got there, he'd took his bike to pieces all over their living-room floor, and he said – Philip, his name is – Phil said as he was going to fix it before he went anywhere, and his mother said he'd better. He said I could help.

So I held spanners and passed parts, and looked at the manual with him, sort of helping him to wish for good luck. He tried to explain it to me, all how the engine worked, but I was never much good at that sort of thing. Got no interest in it. Phil, though, he reads mechanical hand-books like I read *Beano*.

But about half-past seven, even I could see he was in trouble. He decided to leave it for another day. So I helped him move the newspaper, all the bits, bike as well, into his bedroom.

Mrs. Wurnley, Phil's mother, made us some oxtail soup and toast, and we ate it while watching this cowboy on the telly, shouting, 'The Injuns are comin'!' and booing the kissing bits that slow down the brutal killings. Phil's little brother got a toy gun and shot me, so I started creeping round the settee after him, and scalped him, and things got pretty wild after that, when Phil joined in, what with warwhoops and "Bang! Bang! You're dead! No, I'm not. Yes, you are. You missed me. No, I didn't. . . ."

Phil's Mom said we were big saft circus wenches, playing at cowboys and Indians at our age, and that if we didn't sit down and shut up, she wouldn't make any lemonade. So we whipped on to the settee and sat there sniggering, and laughing every time we looked at each other, until Mrs. Wurnley brought in this lemonade she'd made by pouring boiling water on to slices of lemon and sugar. It was smashin'. And they were all so friendly, I never noticed the time going by.

Phil's Dad came in with some Guinness, and we drank it while watching this funny programme about army doctors, Americans, in a war. We never see it at home. When this programme went off, they started, 'BBC 2 is closing down now', and I jumped 'cos I never thought it was that time. I said thanks to everybody and goodbye 'cos I had to go.

When I got in, Dad was annoyed. He wanted to know where I'd been, who with and what had we been doing. He said I deserved a thick ear for staying out that late, and that he'd had to be in by ten o'clock until he was twenty, none of this quarter to twelve business, and he'd been the better for it, and he'd thanked his father for being so strict. I didn't believe a word of it.

Then he said, "Are you drunk?" and I said, "No," because I didn't think I was. I wasn't very steady, and me eyes weren't focusing very well, but when me Dad's drunk he wants to throw his weight about, and I didn't feel like that at all. Fact is, I felt a bit ill, and muzzy, and tired, and I wanted to go to bed.

But Dad started on about honouring your father and mother, telling the truth, and the evils of drink – even though he puts enough of it away. I think he made this point somewhere along the line – "I know I drink, and I know I drink a lot, but that's how I know it does you no good. I don't want you to make the same mistakes as me. Do as I say, not as I do!" And it went on. I sat on the settee while he beat the air round me head. I felt more and more ill until I had to make a dash for the bathroom and throw up in the sink. It was a real good effort. I didn't know I'd eaten that much in the past twenty-four hours. I turned the taps on to clean the sink, feeling sort of weak and shaky, and Dad started up from the hall. He couldn't have thought of a better punishment, and he hoped it would teach me a lesson, and on, and on, and on. Even when I was stood in front of him at the door, waiting to get past, he carried on. In the end, Mom said, "Dick – it's five and twenty to one. You've told him. Let him get to bed now."

Dad glared at her, then at me, and said, "Go on – and you be late for work in the morning, you can look up." Threats, threats.

It was a relief to get back to work. But as things turned out, I'd have done better to stay in bed. It was one of those days. I couldn't do anything right and all day long there were deliveries coming in, and people yelling for me to come and check invoices off, and sign them, and drag in the skips. All day long I was dragging skips; getting me fingers caught between them and the walls; wrestling and sweating to get them into the lift. Then I found I'd forgot me dinner. I was starvin' and all. But Old Claz, he said he'd share his faggots with me. I could buy him a bottle of Scotch for Christmas in return, he said. "'Taint your day, is it, Gramey?" he asked, spooning his dish of faggots into equal parts. "You'm hopeless, you am, hopeless."

After dinner I did some baling to get the great heaps of cardboard out the way and make some room in the back for the big delivery, which arrived before I'd finished. The

Gaffer came to help me, and the two truck-drivers to chuck the stuff out the back of the truck and on to the skips. The skips we shoved into the back, until there was no room for the last one or two, and we had to shove them into the shop. Then me and the Gaffer started to check off the invoices – we had a whole book of them. It was a long, slow business. At half past five, I was good and ready to knock off. I wanted my dinner. I wanted to eat me dinner and then go to bed, and hide from this hard, cruel world where nothing went right for me, and maybe things would be better in the morning. I fetched me jacket from upstairs, and trudged outside.

There was a van by the kerb and this bloke opened the door and jumped out. Great, tall, skinny Indian, he was, with long frizzy hair. "Come on, get in!" he said.

I looked round to see who he was talking to, but there was only me. I'd never laid eyes on him before in me life, I slid away, watching him from the corners of my eyes.

"Come on, give you a lift," he said, surprised that I wasn't interested.

"I don't want a lift," I said.

A head appeared around the door from the back of the van. A white chap. This one said, "Hey-up, Gray, our kid! Old woman Higgins was right then! Her told me you was workin' here." I stared at him, and he said, "Come on, get in!"

He did seem familiar. It took about half a minute for it to sink in that this was Derek, me long lost brother. "It's Derek – isn't it?" He didn't look much like a hippy to me.

"Yeah – come on, get in, we ain't got all day."

The van was crowded. There were three people in the front, besides the driver, two Indian chaps and a wench; and I could hear people talking in the back. "Thanks," I said, "but – I think – "

The other Indian and the girl climbed out of the front, and tipped the seat forward. "Come on," he said.

"Don't be daft, Graeme," Derek said. "Save your bus-

61

fare."

I stooped to get into the van, but then stopped. Besides Derek there were five more men and two girls in the back. "There's no room," I said. "I'll get the bus."

But the Indian shoved me in on top of everybody, and Derek pulled me further in.

"Get your foot off me hand," somebody said.

"Stop kickin'."

The Indians and the girl jumped in, slammed the door, and the big Negro at the wheel started up. I finished up sitting on Derek's knee, holding myself off from the front seat with both hands. Very embarrassing.

"It's wonderful," one of the other men said. "However many people you've crammed into a van, you can always cram more in. That's Singh's law, ain't it, Bob?"

"Yeah," the frizzy-haired Indian said.

"Bed collapses in Smethwick – twenty Pakistanis killed!"

"Fine by me," Bob said. "I'm Indian."

"How do you tell a Jewish house?" the other Indian asked.

Everyone replied in chorus, "By the padlock on the dustbin."

"There's nothing like a spot of race hatred," Derek said. "Do you suppose the wogs and the yids can live in peace now, please?" He told me, "You'll be able to sit down properly when we've dropped some of this lot off, Graeme." He sounded a bit strained, like people are when talking to strangers. Afraid of being disliked. "Long time, no see," he said, and laughed. "It must have been seven years since I've seen him – is it that long? – must be. Seven years."

"Surprised you knew him."

"Oh, he ain't changed all that much."

"He's quiet, I'll give him that," one of the girls said. "Want a fag, love?"

"No thanks," I said.

"Oh – all right." She put one in her own mouth.

"Ain't surprised he's quiet," Derek said, "livin' with his

father and mother. I'll bet they keep you under, eh?"

"I don't know," I said.

"Real bubblin' pot of information, ain't he?"

"He's all right," Derek said.

The van drew into the kerb. Those in front clambered out, and tipped the seat forward. "All ashore who's going ashore." I don't know how many got out, but the van was considerably less crowded when they'd finished. I was able to get off Derek and sit across from him, in a tyre. Then I saw that there was only one girl in the back with us, and the girl from the front had gone. We dropped the other girl off soon after.

I let the van go on for a bit, but then I took to peering anxiously through the windows. "Where are we?" I asked in the end.

"Dudley Road," Derek said.

The Dudley Road. "That's Oldbury."

"We live in Oldbury," Derek said.

"I thought you were going to give me a lift!"

The frizzy-haired Indian turned round and said, "You can come in for a cup of coffee."

"But – " I said.

The Indian gave a big white grin. "I don't think Graeme likes us, Decker."

"It's not that – " I said quickly.

"Come and have some coffee then."

"But me Mom and Dad don't know – they'll worry."

Derek coughed. "Let 'em worry. Won't do 'em any harm. You can't kow-tow to them all your life."

I didn't know what to say without hurting somebody's feelings.

So I sat quiet until the van pulled off the road on to a patch of waste ground between houses. We piled out and shuffled around while the van was locked up, and then we went along the street for two or three houses. They were all tall, old houses with tiny oblongs of overgrown gardens in front. We

63

went up to the door of one. It had a solemn green door with a huge marble knob in the middle. The Negro and the tall Indian pounded with their fists until it was opened by someone unseen.

We huddled through the door, first into a little square room, then into a big hall with red and white tiles and a Gothic staircase, very cold.

"Great to be home," the tall Indian said.

There was a small man, in a pinkish suit, with blue-rinsed hair, who must have let us in. "I was expecting you yesterday."

"We were made so comfortable, we stopped on," Derek said.

"We want coffee," said the other, smaller Indian. "Whose turn is it to make it?"

The big Negro put his hand up. "I made it Friday, I ain't making it." He sloped across the hall and disappeared through this almost hidden, gloomy brown door.

"We're one more than usual," said the small man, spotting me. "Let's not stand about here. It's cold."

"Who's makin' the coffee?"

"Oh – I will," said the small man.

"Good old Dave."

"Come on, let's get in the warm."

We followed the Negro into his sloping-hole. I'd never seen a place like it. It was very small, and brown, because the paintwork was a mixture of dark brown and mustard, and the light from the window was blocked by fossilised net curtains, a calendar showing three dogs and a cat in a basket, a pin-up girl from a newspaper and a list of scores for a card-game. The door, when opened, stuck against a ping-pong table. After you edged round this, you came up against the piano. Then there were six armchairs, of different kinds, packed together arm to arm, front to back, beginning at the piano, and ending at the massive fire-place. Wedged into the corner between the fire-place and the window wall was a television·the size of a goldfish bowl, perched on a small table, with a half-eaten pork-pie on top of it. An alarm-clock ticked on the mantelpiece and the mirror above it was hidden by a paper bell left over from Christmas. The light-bulb had no shade and hung low on its twisted cord, swinging and throwing dark shadows. Pinned to the wall over the tennis-table was a big colour poster of Edward Heath, with a funny hat drawn on him in crayon, a big red nose and a joke flower. Over the piano were two posters, one of a nude girl on a lion, and the other of a bloke all done up in leather on a motor-bike.

Seeing me hesitate, the tall Indian half-bowed and said, "Come in, Graeme! Sit by the fire, take off your coat, be at home – don't worry about the chairs – climb over them." Derek and the other Indian were jumping from arm to seat. I sat on the arm of the nearest chair. The tall Indian grinned and said, "We must be friendly, eh, Graeme? We must have the introductions." He wore a denim jacket and jeans, and was very Western-like, but he still had that very serious, overdone politeness that marked him out as foreign. "I," he said, "am Barjhinder Singh, but they call me Bob. This is my brother Ron, and that – " he pointed to the big Negro, "is Alec. The man who makes the coffee is David. This is a lodging house, you see, owned by my parents, who are now in London. We have just come back from visiting them." He held out his hand and I solemnly shook it. Ron, Derek and Alec were all watching the foggy television screen. Bob climbed into the chair beside me and kept conversation going. "We were just on our way to London when Decker says, man, stop here, our kid works here, and we went in and asked for you but they said you'd gone. So when we were coming back, he says, let's see if we can catch him this time – do you play table-tennis?"

I said I did, so we started to play, and the telly-watchers turned up the volume. I don't know how far away the kitchen was, but we'd played two games before there was a knocking on the door behind me. I opened it as far as it would go, and the little man came in with the coffee on a tray. But I wanted my dinner.

"David!" Bob said. "David, this is Graeme, Derek's brother."

David put the coffee down, grabbed my hand and shook it. I'd never had my hand shook so much before. "Yes," he said. "You look like Derek."

I was startled into half-turning round to see Derek. He was a bigger man than me father, taller, and his hair was fairer than mine, more like Mother's. I couldn't figure out how anyone could think we looked alike.

"Pleased to meet you, Graeme," this David said.

"An'–an' me," I mumbled.

"Do you take sugar? Good, because I've sugared them all." He put a mug of coffee into my hand. "Sit down, Graeme," Bob said. "Be comfortable, man."

I perched on the chair arm again and fixed my eyes on the television. I was wondering how soon I could get out of this. I wanted to go home and have my dinner. But I didn't like asking for a lift, or just up and leaving.

There was this old film on, about huge poisonous plants from Mars running riot all over the place, and we watched it through to the bitter end. They were good company really, friendly and making these jokes about the film, laughing all the time. I should have enjoyed being there if it hadn't been for thinking about Mom and Dad not knowing where I was. When the film went off, I coughed, and said, "Will there be a bus to Dudley soon?"

"What's this about buses?" Ron Singh said.

I pushed at the hair that hung in my eyes. "I've got to be goin'."

"Don't bother about buses, man," Bob said. "I'll give you a lift in a bit. Sit down, be comfortable. There's just this thing on I want to see. . . ." When it went off it must have been nearly nine o'clock. I didn't like to *ask* for a lift,

66

although I was hoping I would get one. "I shall *have* to go now," I said.

"You'll stay for another cup of coffee," Bob said, and when I hesitated, "Hey, don't rush off – we *like* you, man, you're right down our street!"

"I want me dinner," I said, pathetically like.

Alec, the big Negro, suddenly rose up from his armchair, where he'd been slumped all night. "Yeah, dinner. This place is like a bloody monastery." He glared round at us.

"Fish and chips?" Ron suggested, but Bob killed this. "We had chips last night. Fed up of these and they're bloody expensive too."

"There's some beans," the little blue-rinsed bloke said. "And I think you'll find some potatoes if you look hard enough. And some eggs, but they might be bad."

"I'll eat anything," Derek said, "so long as Bob doesn't cook it."

"I think Derek should cook it, if he doesn't like *my* cooking," Bob said. This was passed with cheers and whistles.

"It couldn't be worse than if Bob cooked it," Derek said, and got up, came jumping across people and chairs to the door. "Graeme – come on. You'm cook's assistant, and chief bottle-washer."

"But – " I said.

"You can stop and have summat to eat," they said. "Don't go just yet. We'll give you a lift in a minute."

Derek tapped my shoulder, and I followed him out into the chilly hall. My footsteps clattered. The hall went on, with its red and white tiles, for miles, very dark and gloomy, like a stately home. I wasn't surprised it had taken so long to get the coffee. We passed doors to four other rooms before we reached the kitchen. Derek opened the door and snapped on the light, which was dim yellow. The kitchen was yellow too: mustard yellow. It was a big room, with a table marooned in the centre, with one chair. Under the window was a heavy square sink, with all its ugly pipes showing, a bit indecent,

67

and a sloping wooden draining-board clinging to the wall. The floor was a mixture of red tile, green lino and scruffy rugs. There was a greasy, dirty gas-stove tucked up one corner, and a cupboard high in the centre of one wall. Placed across the far corner, by the door into the yard, was a sideboard. Every flat surface, the floor as well, was piled with empty cans, mainly baked-bean cans. And everything, sink, stove, table, sideboard, cupboard and cans, seemed tiny compared to the room.

"The bathroom's in there," Derek said, pointing to a door opening off the kitchen. Curiously, I wandered over and opened the door, looked in. It was a room half the size of the kitchen, but still big, that had been converted into a bathroom. Three and a half of the walls were a sullen, scowling green, and half a wall was bright orange. Tins of paint and brushes, rollers and a pair of step-ladders cluttered the place up.

Derek was opening the wall cupboard when I turned back into the kitchen. "Have a look in the sideboard, see if you can find anythin'."

I opened the doors of the sideboard and breathed in the smell of damp sugar, damp tea, old, damp newspapers, and just general damp. The shelves were covered with newspaper, but not much else. I took out, and placed on the floor, two big tins of baked beans.

"I've got the eggs," Derek said. "What is there?" He came over and joined me in peering into the cupboard. "Hey!" he said, and reached into the dark recesses, pulled out nearly a full gallon jar of cider. "We'll get some of this down we, Graeme, our kid."

"I should be getting home."

"Ah, home, shome. Give over moaning and enjoy our hospitality. Some cheese there, pass that cheese. Scrape everything into the frying pan and serve. We live on scrape-ups. Some bread, ain't there? I hope there is – oh." The bread was on top of the sideboard. Derek assembled all the ingredients of the meal on the table, looked at them, and said, "Let's have a drink first." He reached up into the wall cupboard, took down two tall glasses, and filled them to the top with cider.

I drank the cider and watched Derek, thinking. I seemed to be looking at two people at once. I knew he was my brother, and my brother had been somebody who'd sat on me bed to keep the dark away, and teased me into crying by persuading me that he'd bitten both my ears off; who used to swing me round in circles until I couldn't stand up, and pretend to be a duck, so I'd feed him my sweets, and who took me for rides on the handle-bars of his bike. Me brother didn't seem to have much to do with this tall thin bloke in his sweatshirt and jeans, with his scrubby fair hair and narrow beard. This bloke was a stranger, and I was shy of him. I think he was shy too, he talked so fast.

"Them 'taters – we'll shove 'em in the oven and roast 'em, that'll be easier than anythin' else. They am clean, ain't they? Good, good. And fried eggs, I suppose. Get a saucer, here – " he reached down a saucer – "and crack them eggs, see if they'm bad."

I took another swig of cider, which was another of the mistakes I made that day. I always thought of cider as a kind of pop, soft drink. It isn't. I cracked the eggs while Derek lit the oven. He fetched a can-opener from the sideboard, came back, and refilled the glasses before opening the beans. "You'll find some saucepans and a pan under the stove. And a fish-fry."

I swept the old cans away from in front of the stove, and hauled the pans from beneath it, making tracks through the deep grease. Crouching by the stove, I doled a lump of fat into the frying pan from the fish-fry, using the fish-slice. I took the pan and a big saucepan over to the table. With an elegant twist of his wrists, Derek emptied the cans into the saucepan. "Voilà!" I grinned, and he laughed. "You won't be hungry when you've got this lot inside you. Sick, maybe,

69

but never hungry."

I drained the glass of cider, got the eggs on to fry. Derek lit the grill and produced an old biscuit-tin lid. "Put 'em on there and shove 'em under the grill when they'm done. Here – come here – put the slice down and take this." He put the glass into my hand and filled it with cider. "How long does it take 'taters to roast?"

"Twenty minutes?" I guessed.

"They'm goin' to keep the rest waitin'. Never mind." He put the beans on. "Cheers." Smacked his lips and said, "Maybe we can afford summat a bit stronger than cider. After all, it's a celebration – family reunion."

I dropped the egg on to the biscuit lid and shoved it under the grill. "Ye-ah," I said, on a nervous laugh, but I'd have been happier if it had been a real family reunion.

He'd got the cider jar again. "Come on, drink that." He waited impatiently while I emptied the glass, then refilled it. "You'm nifty with the eggs, my son. Put the kettle on – it's on the draining board."

I filled it, and he lit the gas for it, and put the tea into the tea-pot. I cracked and fried eggs.

Then we had the beans and eggs done, and were waiting on the potatoes. Derek wrapped a tea-towel round his hands and pulled them out – they were also on a biscuit-lid. He prodded them with a fork and said that they were hard in the middle. So he sat on the one chair, and I sat on the table, and we drank more cider. I was beginning to feel – not drunk – but a bit blurred.

"Well," Derek said. He grinned up at me. "How you goin' on, kid?"

"All right," I said.

"How's Mom and Dad? I know you think I ought to ask."

"They're – all right," I said.

He sniggered. "Fill up the glasses, kidder. Go on, fill 'em, don't give half measure. I mean, is Dad still his same old lovable self?"

"I suppose so," I said.

"Start again," he said. "How you doin', kid? Like your job?"

"Oh ar, it's all right," I said. The 'all right' was beginning to irritate him, so I hurriedly tried to enlarge. "I mean, I like them I work with. Some nice, good-looking girls, I can tell you – and Old Claz, he's a good un. They'm all friendly like. But the job's a bit boring. I mean, some of it's all right, but the stackin' and packin'-in, you get fed up of that. The place is a bit – well – a bit – " I moved my hands together. "Like bein' shut in all the while."

"Claustrophobic."

"Stuffy. I'd like to work in the park. I'd like to work outside and in a park there'd be plants – see, I like to grow things. In pots. I got a cactus is going to flower."

He listened close to what I said. If I try to tell Claz, or the Gaffer, or Mom or Dad about somethin' that I've found funny, or interestin', they don't listen. They say, "Yes, yes – " and they'm doin' something else all the while. And I can hear my own voice getting more and more worked up with this false excitement, trying to attract their attention, until it's downright embarrassing. And they still don't listen. You can tell they're not listening.

Now Derek said, "You should pack in your job and get one outside." I don't think even he was really serious, until I said, "I was thinking about it."

"Oh. You really are fed up of your job then?"

"Yeah. I just said so."

"Well, go on then," Derek said. "Don't carry on and carry on until you stagnate and can't do anything."

I sat, turning the glass between my hands, and saying nothing.

"Ah," Derek said, and put his own glass on the table with a 'tump'. "Dad won't like it."

"No, he won't."

"This is old ground," Derek said. "Super-Dad strikes

71

again! Well, it's your life, not his. It's fine for him – he likes his job. He doesn't go day after day to a place he dislikes – hates. Don't let him run things for you, because he will if you let him. Pack it in."

I tried to explain the fear I had, fear of making Dad angry. I was really afraid of making him angry, but not even I could explain very clearly why. I wasn't scared that he'd welt me; I knew he wouldn't. Then there's only the lectures he gives, and who can be afraid of a telling-off? It's only words, and words never hurt anybody. Sticks and stones. . . . I think it's something like fear of the guilt his words make in me. They make me guilty because he is finding fault in me and it hurts him; I know that he loves me and means the best. But I could never *say* that. The piss that would be took out of me if I said something like that! I said, "I've got Mom to ask him about me leavin' this job I've got. Her's goin' to ask him today."

Derek was quiet for a bit. "He won't say 'yes', you know. I'll tell you that for nothin'. He'll be dead against it just because it's *your* idea. That's why. That's how it was with me. Any idea I had, he had to stamp on. If I said any film even, or book, or anything was good – he had to tear it to pieces, because that was *my* opinion. He'll find a thousand good reasons why you shouldn't change your job, but I'd bet you my last quid that if we could open him up and see his nasty little mind ticking away there, the real reason he'd be against it is because it's *your* idea. You're not supposed to have a mind of your own. You're supposed to go around holding his hand all your life. 'Daddy, Daddy, please take me to the bog, Daddy.' I really hate his guts. He used to get up my nose! I think there was times I could have killed him, I mean it. *Everything* I did and thought, he had to block it. Trying to browbeat me to his way of thinking. And then my friends didn't suit him, and I was wasting my time reading. I came in too late, I shouldn't drink – him, with his beer-belly! I tell you, he – " He didn't finish the sentence. He sat there, his lips turned in, his face three or four shades paler. He was livid, as they say. He took another drink and relaxed a bit. "I just decided I couldn't stand any more, an' that if I wanted to live me own life without having a bloody show-down at the O.K. Corral every time I wanted to go out or have a drink, I'd got to get out and leave him to fight with his finger-ends. Bob's parents have run this place for years. Cheap. One word and I was in, shared room, but better than having *him* on your back all the while. I'm glad I left. Really glad." He took another drink. "I've often wondered how you was getting on with him."

"We get on all – fine," I said.

"Yeah, you do, until you start thinking for yourself."

Neither of us said anything after that. We sat and listened to the gas jets in the oven. The silence grew fidgety. "What do you do now then?" I asked.

"What do I do? Job, you mean? I ain't got a job at the moment." He laughed. "I'm decorating the bathroom to pay me rent. Oh – I work on and off, when I can get a job, and when I want to – let's face it, most of the time, I just have to get a job – but I'll tell you this, I never stick a job when I'm fed up on it. I throw it up."

"Just like that?"

"Yeah! There's always another. Mind, they ain't cushy numbers like yours. But any old mucky un'll do. My needs are frugal. I save up a bit, then give notice. Meanwhile, back at the rancho, there's nobody dictating how late I shall stay up, what I will read, how much I shall drink –. I go walkabout sometimes. Just – well, like a tramp. I come back here. Travel! See the world! And you do. You can meet some funny people that way, son. Widens your experience. It did mine."

Blimey. He *was* a hippy. I sat on the corner of the table and stared at him. I was trying to will him into telling me about the 'funny' people he'd met. I didn't like to just ask. I was hoping he'd up and tell me.

He said, "Ever read *The Perfumed Garden*?"

"No," I said.

"I'll lend it to you when I get it back. A bloody lendin' library, I am. Shall have to start charging for overdue books."

"Thanks," I said. I don't mind reading gardening books, even though we haven't got a garden. And I like scented plants. You can grow a lot of 'em in small pots, like herbs.

He filled his glass again, and stretched back in his chair. "Any time you want to clear out, you know," he said, "you can move in here. Bob'll let you. He's the landlord now. His Mom and Dad am in London. He bends the rules a bit."

"I'm all right!" I said. "I don't want to leave home."

"Well, I didn't at first, but I'm glad I did. It became plain that freedom, democracy and Our Dad couldn't exist in the same house. We used to hate one another like poison. We'd fight like cat and dog."

"He don't hate you," I said. "He's always wishin' you'd come and see us." He looked doubting. "'S truth," I told him. I was hoping he would come and see us. Then Phil and me other mates could meet him.

"Well, he can wish in one hand and piss in the other, see which gets full the quickest."

"That ain't fair," I said. On Mom, or something, I meant.

He understood what I meant. "Look – if I went, we'd only fight. We can't agree. We're diametrically opposite. Plus and negative. He's Tory, I'm Labour. He thinks a 'Good Man' touches his cap and works his life away. 'A good day's work for a good day's pay.' I believe a Good Man finds his own way of life without hurting others, or – well, degrading himself. Work is degrading. Using *your* time, spending your life, for somebody else's gain. I've got this idea I might try to work one day. Get some people together, scrape up some money, buy some land up in Scotland – farm for ourselves. A commune. That'd be great. All the work'd be for *us*, see. Just for us."

"You could never do it," I said.

He looked dreamily (drunkenly?) past me, and said, "Oh,

74

you could, you could – where was I? Yeah, wasting your life for people you don't know. When – when the last trump is blown and it's all over, where will me and Dad be? Six feet under, son, that's where. But who'll have put their life to the most use? Who'll have the most experience, eh?"

"You ought to see the foundry," I said. "When they pour the metal out all like water – it's great!"

"Exactly," Derek said. "I say 'experience', and to you, 'experience' plus Dad equals 'foundry'. All he knows. Never a day off in twenty-four, thirty or however many years it is, oh Christ, the potatoes!"

They were blackened, I got off the table to help, and found I was a good deal drunker than I'd thought. Derek dealt out plates, and served a potato on to each with quick, scorched fingers. "Butter!" he said. "We need butter. Have a look in the sideboard."

I missed the sideboard by an inch or two and had to try again. I found the butter in one of the drawers eventually, and by that time Derek had served the eggs and beans. "Right," he said, "we'll be a bit crafty, me and you. We'll take our dinners and make the rest of 'em troop down 'ere. Then we'll get the best chairs. Take any one." He rattled in the sideboard drawers. "Here's a knife and fork. You take the butter, and I'll bring the bread and salt."

I led the way back up the hall, balancing the knife and fork on the plate, and I kept turning round to see Derek, and laughing at him. I was a bit drunk. He was having trouble with the plate, the big drum of salt, and the loaf under his arm. "I'll give it thee, laughin' at me in a minute!" He laughed so that his voice rang off the dark ceiling upstairs. He was drunk too.

I couldn't open the living-room door. "Kick it," Derek said, so I did, and behold, it opened. We edged in, and put the things on the ping-pong table. "You'll have to go and get yours," Derek said. They groaned and moaned and struggled past us. "Quick," Derek said, "into Alec's chair." I

75

bounced over the armchairs to the farthest one, nearest the window and the telly. It was old, broken-down and comfortable. "Butter!" Derek called. "Catch! Salt – catch! Here's your dinner – watch it! Don't want baked beans in the chairs. Here, hold mine a minute." I held his dinner while he clambered into the next chair. He settled down, and then said, "Sod it! We left the bread behind!" He stared longingly at the bread on the green tennis-table as if it was a mile away.

Bob, David and Ron came back with their dinners and the cider, what was left of it. They were cautious about approaching their dinners. "I think Bob could have done better," David said. But I didn't care if the eggs were rubbery, the beans – peculiar, and the potatoes burnt. I was hungry, and then I was tired, and I wanted me bed. Bob had said he'd give me a lift after. I didn't like to remind him, after he'd fed me and everything.

Alec came rolling in with a pack of six Guinnesses. Strong stuff that Guinness. "I wonder what Guinness and cider are like?" Derek said. I was watching the telly with watering eyes and people were talking. It was a warm, nice sort of noise to listen to.

The alarm clock went off, and I was befuddled for a bit, but then jumped up, reaching out of bed for it. "Hey, hey, hey," a voice said. "Don't start on me." I blinked. A strange room and a collection of strange, hairy blokes.

Bob was standing up, with the alarm clock from the mantelpiece, winding it up. Derek held down my reaching arm that had belted him across the gob. I retreated into my own chair and rubbed my face, pushing my hair back from my brow.

"You went to sleep," Derek said. "Can't take your drink."

"Oh." I thought: bloody hell – it must be ten by now. "I got to get home," I said.

"At this time?" Derek asked. Ron yawned.

"What time is it?" I asked, a bit scared.

76

"Two o'clock in the mornin'," Bob said. "Someone had the clock set for two this afternoon, so not to miss the two-thirty at Chepstow."

"Two o'clock in the morning!" My head felt dizzy and heavy. "Oh Christ."

"You can sleep here tonight," Derek said.

"Or rather, you can carry on sleeping here tonight." Bob put the clock back with a big white smile.

"What about Mom and Dad?"

"His Mom and Dad, his Mom and Dad," Bob said, grinning.

"Bugger 'em," Derek said. He stood up. "Come on, Aynoch." I got up stiffly and blundered after him. "They'll be worried."

"Tough luck."

And I was too tired to argue.

The end room, nearest the kitchen, was Derek's. I only saw the bed. I started to undress, pulled me jumper off, took off me trousers. Me fingers fumbled on the shirt buttons and I thought, What the Hell, and crawled in as I was. The light was switched out.

The morning came in a warm, strong, sweaty-smelling fug. I was half-buried and could hardly move. I worked one arm out and pushed the blankets back from my face, picked sleep out of my eyes. I yawned and dozed. It was dark and I struggled to sit up, but couldn't. There was a groaning above me, a muttering, and I flopped back.

I was in bed with two other people. I was in the middle, in the hollow that all old beds get, and them on either side of me had nearly rolled on top of me. I fought harder and managed to shove up between the two snorers, closing my eyes as a sudden dart of pain shot through my head. My head felt as if it was stuffed with layers and layers of thick cloth. I didn't feel very clever at all.

I sat between these two blanket-covered hummocks, one elbow on each lump, and my head in my hands. "What time is it?" I asked, and got no answer.

It occurred to me to find out just who I was dossing with. You can't be too careful these days. So I pulled back the blankets from the smaller lump. It was Derek. The other hump was much bigger, and snored, and shuddered. The face beneath the blanket was red and damp and fat. God above knows who he was, but he stank of sweat and beer.

"What time is it?" I asked again, and shook Derek. Not a murmur.

Well, I had to get up, if nobody else did. I heaved myself out of the trough, and rolled over Derek, pulled on my trousers and jumper. There were no windows, so I couldn't guess the time by the light.

I went out into the hall. I could hear someone talking somewhere, but I could see that the kitchen was empty because the door was open, and there was no one in the hall. I clattered down the tiles to the living-room and went in. It was murky and brown and smelt of beer. Dirty plates and cups stood on the table. I found the alarm clock in an armchair. It was still going, and it said twenty past eight. Oh bloody hell, twenty past eight! I was supposed to be at work by half-past.

I was jittery. I didn't know what to do. Before dropping off to sleep I'd had some hazy idea of getting up early and going to explain to Mom and Dad before work, but now I hadn't time. And the longer I stood biting my thumb with a feeling like bubbling inside, the less time I had.

What to do?

I had to get to work. And to tell the truth, I wasn't very keen to do the explaining to my parents. They wouldn't worry very much, I thought. They know I'm old enough to look after myself. It'll do tonight. I'd tell 'em that I would have come, but I had to go to work. Dad'll see that. It'll be all right.

The kitchen door banged, echoing in the hall. I found my jacket hanging on the stair-post, and went through to the

78

front door. I could just reach the top bolt, and I slammed the door behind me and raced down the road, pulling on me jacket.

I found a bus-stop and hopped about beside it, looking at my watch and biting at my thumb. At half past eight I ran on to the next stop, and joined a queue of women. I licked my lips, panting and gasping. The bus came at nearly quarter to nine. As I reached into my pocket for the fare, the doubts come again. I was going to be so late for work anyway, wouldn't it be better to go home first? But I didn't want to go home –

"Come on, son, be 'ere till Christmas," the conductor said.

"Ahm – how much to Dudley from here?"

"Twelve and half pence."

"Tw-twelve and half." I put ten pence into his hand and delved in my pocket for the rest. The conductor checked them carefully, as if he suspected me of trying to cheat him, threw the coins contemptuously into his satchel and cranked me out a ticket. I sat on the edge of my seat, folding and rubbing the ticket, willing the bus to go faster and not stop so often.

At ten past nine, the bus pulled into the terminal at the bottom of Dudley, by the 'Empire' pub. I got up uncertainly. "Is this as far as you go?"

"Go to Oldbury."

"Now?"

"Yeah! Oldbury to Dudley an' back, this."

"Hang on then! I'm off here." I swung off the bus and ran along its length as it pulled away, dodging behind it. The bus terminal is a big, cobbled circle, with concrete shelters and platforms around the edges. I ran across the cobbles, and my heart was nearly stopped by the blare of the hooter. I skipped back from the wheels of the bus as it swept by me. The conductor leaned out and yelled something. I ran on.

I ran uphill from one end of the town to the other; along

79

the new shopping precinct, feet echoing in the early morning emptiness, across the street and past Woollies, up the cobbled alleyway to the High Street, and all uphill past the bank, past the shoe shops, past the arcade, and the new shopping centre, and still on, right to the top of the town. I finally fell through the doors of the shop just after quarter past nine, forty-five minutes late. Even in a state of advanced exhaustion, my low animal cunning still works. I merged with a clump of customers, and went round behind them, hidden by the shelves. The inter-com crackled and cut through the taped music. "Mr. Bowen to the office, please."

I just couldn't win.

4

I broke into a weary trot round the shelves to the doors into the back. "Late, ain't yer, Gray?" Claz asked. I nodded and leaned on the swing-doors. Claz winked as I fell through.

The Gaffer was facing the open door, waiting for me, as I plodded up his office steps. He looked at his watch. "What time do you call this?"

I stood awkwardly in the office doorway, one elbow in the air, pulling at me hair with one hand. "I'm sorry I'm late, sir, but I overslept and I missed the bus."

"I don't know," he said. "All right – get out o' me sight."

I thumped down the office steps and squeezed between the skips to get upstairs. After changing into me overall I nipped into the Male Persons' Toilet, used the bog, washed my face, and tried to comb my hair into some sort of order with my fingers. I looked at myself in the mirror, thin and pale, spotty-faced with a mass of floppy brown hair hanging down into washed-out blue eyes that were a bit fishy. I wondered what me Mom and Dad were thinking about me at that moment. It worried me. I suddenly felt that I'd done the wrong thing, I should have took the day off and gone home, confessed all, tried to patch it all up. I felt that I was rushing along a conveyor belt straight into a quarry, and there was no way off. I couldn't go home until tonight now.

I went downstairs and back into the Gaffer's office to fetch the stock-cards. As I reached across the desk for 'em, I tried very hard to ignore the Gaffer, and act as if I wasn't in disgrace for being three-quarters of an hour late. But in the end I slid him an apologetic look. He was smiling. "If them ain't done by half five, you can stop on till quarter past six to finish 'em."

"Fair enough," I said.

It was about ten o'clock, when I was sitting cross-legged on top of a skip, filling in a stock-card, that the bell to the loading-door rang long and loud. I came up to one knee, but carried on writing. The bell rang again. "All right!" I shouted, but the bell went on, in short jabs, buzz, buzz, buzz. "All *right*!" I yelled, threw down the card and jumped from skip to skip, slithered off the last one, and went to answer the door. Even though I was shouting right against the door, the ringing went on. I flipped off the catch and started to pull. The door's very heavy and stiff, and I have to take hold of the handle with both hands and throw all my weight on it, slowly pulling myself upright as the door grumbles back. When I stuck my head out, it was a truckful of sugar. I know the driver well, he comes every week; heavy-built, smiling bloke with three days' growth of beard. It takes me three weeks to grow that much. He gave me a big smile. "Hello, youth."

"Hello, chap," I said.

"Ready to help me get this lot in?" he asked.

I glanced behind me at all the jam-packed skips. "There ain't much room – I think you'll have to help me get some upstairs."

"Wh-a-t?" He came bustling in. "Ah, we can get it in here. Come on." We fetched skips from upstairs in the lift, and threw the sugar out of the van, twenty-eight-pound parcels, swung from him to me, and I packed 'em neatly on the skip. He rolled up his sleeves, ready to give me a hand shoving the skip inside. I set my shoulder against the edge of the loading-door, and slid it the rest of the way back. "Well, come on, youth," he said. I took hold of either side of the skip, leaned back, and braced my feet. "Ready?"

"Ar," he said.

I pulled, he pushed, and the skip lurched forward. I pushed sideways to turn it in through the door. Then it stuck. I gritted my teeth and pulled until I could feel every separate bone of my back pressing out against me skin, and me guts had wound into a hard ball. But the skip wasn't moving. The driver yelled from the other side, "Come on! Pull! You ain't trying."

I panted, and licked my lips, set my feet again. A policeman suddenly came through the door beside the skip. Coppers do come for shop-lifters, but I hadn't noticed any shop-lifters. I wondered what he'd come for, leaned back and pulled.

"You'm leavin' me to do all the work, youth!" the driver called. "Idle lay-about. Pull!"

The copper slapped my shoulder, and jerked his thumb over his shoulder. He went through the doors into the shop, and I went around the skip. The driver was standing with his feet lodged in the sugar-parcels, shouting for all he was worth, "Come on, youth! Pull!"

I leaned on the corner of the skip. "Ha, ha, bloody ha," I said. "What about you doin' some work? We haven't got all day."

"Ooh, what's up with thee? Mardy this morning, aren't we?"

"Aah, belt up and get shovin'."

He clenched a fist under my nose. "Want a slice of knuckle pie?"

"Sod off."

"Cheeky little bugger, aren't yer?"

"You'm no bloody oil-painting yourself," I said. He was one of those blokes who'm all smiles one minute, but turn very touchy if they think they'm gettin' the mickey took out of 'em. His big hairy fist was right under me nose and I could see all the cracks round these big knuckles. But I wasn't going to act scared of him – that was what he wanted.

"Somebody wants to give you a clip round the lug."

"It won't be thee." It was getting to be a close-run thing as to whether we'd be moving the skip or squaring up to each other in the next few minutes. If he wanted a fight, I'd give him one. Even though I'd get a belting. I'd put one right in his flabby chops first. But he was saved from this by the Gaffer yelling, "Graeme!"

I jumped, and turned round. The Gaffer was at the door of his office. He waved his hand and said, "Come here quick!"

The quickest way was to go into the shop through the double doors, run past the fruit-counter, and in through the smaller door at the foot of the office-steps. I could get round the skips that way. I ran up into the office. The copper was sitting on one of the stools. "This is Graeme Bowen," the Gaffer said to the copper.

The copper swivelled round and looked at me from under his peaked cap like I was something not worth the money he'd paid for it. "You're Graeme Bowen, eighty-seven, Ward House, Pine Road, Pleck Estate, Dudley?"

I coughed. "Yeah. That's right."

The copper nodded slowly, a man who'd got nothing less than he'd expected. "And where d'you think you've been all night, worrying your mother to death?"

I glanced at the Gaffer, who was looking very grim. I didn't want to go into long explanations, or really to say anything at all. Finding nowhere to look, I looked down.

"Your mother's given we gyp," said the copper. "Seems to think it's *our* fault you didn't go home last night. They've been wanting helicopters circlin', and every canal between here and Brum dragged –" His imagination ran out, and he said, "We've got cars and coppers out just lookin' for *you*." I don't know whether this was true or not, but it made me feel guilty, so it wasn't wasted. He tilted his radio to his mouth and sent a message back to the station, saying that I'd been found, safe and sound at work. There came back a crackle and buzz that I couldn't understand, but he could, because he said, "No, not a care in the world. Happy as a sand-boy – There'll be a copper round to your Mom and Dad to tell 'em the wanderer's been found." He stood up and suddenly jabbed a finger at me. "You're *lucky*, my lad. An hour late and your Mom and Dad were looking for you, half-nine and they were through to us." He half-turned to the Gaffer. "We had a case, and when the mother reported the kid missin', the last time she'd seen him had been *three* days before. Said her'd thought he was with friends – but hadn't bothered to check! He wasn' as old as this one either. When we found him, had to take him to hospital. Exposure. You ought to be thankful as you've got a Mom an' Dad that care about you, my lad, not go off, worryin' 'em sick." My face was as red and hot as a gas-fire. "Eh?" said the copper. "Eh?" I gave a sort of nod, or shake, or movement of me head.

The Gaffer was annoyed, and so spoke very quietly and politely. "Excuse me, Officer, but mightn't it be best for Graeme to go home now – put his mother's mind at rest?" He frowned at me. "Get it all over and done with."

The policeman put on his cap. "I'll give him a lift, Gaffer, if it's all right by you."

The Gaffer nodded. "Go and get your coat, Graeme." Nobody asked me what I wanted to do.

But without a murmur I did as I was told, and then followed the copper out into the yard. The truck-driver watched us go in surprise, but managed to say, "I always knowed you'd come to a sticky end." I didn't think it very funny at the time.

The copper got into his panda-car, and opened the passenger door for me. I got in and slammed the door. "Put your safety-belt on," he said, and turned the ignition while I fumbled with the buckle. As the car moved out, he said, "Next stop Ward House." I wished he hadn't said that. The car pulled on to the High Street and turned uphill towards the church. I worked sweaty fingers together with anxiety.

85

"Why did you go off?" the copper asked.

My throat was so tight it hurt, and I nervous, jumpy. "I didn't mean to!"

"You didn't mean to? Did you lose your memory? Or get lost? Or catch the wrong bus – your Mom told me every bus that you can catch to get home, which stop you catch 'em at, which stop you get off at, *and* the times they leave and arrive!"

I giggled, but it was nerves, not the joke. I started to bite at my thumb, then snatched it from my mouth, and pushed both hands between my thighs.

"Well?" the copper asked. "How come you didn't mean to go off?"

"I went with me brother – me brother Derek." I felt sick. In a twisted way I knew Dad was going to think my 'going off' was worse because I'd gone with Derek; because he was my brother and their son. I took a deep breath, trying to get some control over the shaking inside me.

The copper said, "Would it have hurt to have told 'em you was going to see him?"

I shook my head. "I didn't know. Him and his mates – they picked me up outside the shop, was going to give me a lift, but I went for a cup of coffee with 'em first. They said, 'Don't go for the bus.'" I stopped and did some more deep breathing. The longer I heard my explanation going on, the more sure I was that Mom and Dad weren't going to be convinced. I was sick with apprehension but I didn't know why – I wasn't going to get a hiding – Dad wouldn't even raise his voice, I *knew*. But just the same, I was scared sick and I was biting, really biting at me thumb again. "Don't bother with the bus, they said, we'll give you a lift, and then they kept puttin' it off, and we had some to drink and I went to sleep, and then it was too late an' I couldn't go home this morning 'cos I had to go to work." And my thumb suffered again. Blood began to seep out around the nail and I sucked it away.

"There's a list of mistakes," the copper said. "Bit of a farce, ain't it? Your Mom and Dad aren't going to be pleased with you, are they? I know mine wouldn't have been."

"No," I said.

He threw me a quick glance as the car turned a corner. "Oh come on, buck up. It's not the end of the world, is it? What're they going to do – shoot you?" He frowned and looked thoughtful. "Er – I suppose it *will* be all right – you know?" I said nothing, and he went on after a bit, "It'll be all right. Some shoutin' and cussin' but that never hurt anybody an' – it's because they care about you, you know." He had difficulty saying this and I'm not surprised. I mean, they always say things like that, and it just doesn't figure, does it? You're worried about somebody, scared they might be hurt, they say, so when they come back and they're not hurt, all Hell's let loose. It doesn't figure. If I was worried about somebody and scared they might be hurt, I'd be *glad* when they come back safe. I wouldn't put 'em through it.

"Yeah," I said to him. He didn't know, and it wasn't him that was going to have to live with my Mom and Dad for the next few weeks. The car pulled up outside Ward House, and I looked out of the window at it. I didn't want to go in. I was going to tip into the quarry if I moved. I kept sitting there, making no offer to get out, just hanging on, you know, a few more peaceful seconds.

"Shall I come up with you for a bit?" the copper asked. "That'll keep everybody sweet for a bit, a stranger in the house."

I didn't have any hopes like that. I knew that his going in with me would make matters worse in the finish. But I was a real coward. "If you like," I said.

The copper got out, so then I had to. I was glad to wait while he locked up. We then began the slow march up to the door. It was terrible. And waiting for the lift set me shivering. I was chewing away at the skin round me nail like I hadn't eaten for weeks.

87

Inside the lift I watched the floors counting off, swallowing my sickness. The fifteenth floor.

"Here we are," the copper said cheerfully. He led the way across the hall to the door of our flat, and knocked. I stood behind him and heard the door open. "Oh," my mother said, "what –"

The copper stepped aside, too quick for me to keep with him, and left me out in the open with nowhere to hide. I saw my mother's face harden and close. "He's back, Mrs. Bowen. May I come in a minute?"

The copper ushered me in, as if he owned the place, and sat down. He launched himself into an explanation of why I'd not come home. He did his best, but Mother nodded and smiled, and ignored every word. I stood behind the settee and she never looked or spoke to me. I kept wishing the copper would go. He meant well, but he was only making it worse. I'd have to pay for all of it. With every word, Mother's smile grew sweeter, but inside her that sweetness was stewing and converting into poison, like sunlight into chloro-whatsit inside a leaf.

In the end he picked up his cap, and Mother showed him out. I walked slowly round and sat on the settee. I heard Mother being nice to the copper at the door, and clenched sweaty hands together, waiting for her to come. But after she'd shut the door, she went into the kitchen. I could hear her moving things about, banging and chinking. I began to wish she'd come and bawl me out, and have done. I wondered about going and saying – what – 'I'm sorry'? That really would do it! Better to let her get on with it her own way. Slow and painful, like the ancient Chinese water torture. She began singing to show *she* didn't care.

She came in from the kitchen, still singing and ignoring me, but the singing soon died away. In silence she viciously straightened cushions. A neat touch – she was wearing the shell-necklace, and it screamed at me louder than she ever could. She came and stood close by, looking into the mirror on the wall beside the settee. She pushed at her hair and said, "I suppose we should be grateful you've come home at all."

Here we went then.

"I hope you enjoyed yourself. Your father and I had a wonderful time, all night, worrying about where you were."

She turned and strolled away, leaving behind a smell of washing-powder and fruit-cake from her apron. "Of course, *you* don't care. You don't care if we were worried to death, not knowing where you were or what had happened to you. You don't care. So long as you can selfishly enjoy *yourself*, you don't care."

Oh God. She could go on for hours.

She spun round on her heels and yelled, "What do you think you were playing at? Haven't you got any sense at all? Don't you know any better? What a stupid bloody thing to do! I know what you want, and by God, if you were a year or two younger you'd cop it, my lad! I'd start on you and I wouldn't know when to stop!" She paused for breath, panting a bit, then she paced up and down, working herself into a fury, pulling at the shoulder of her dress. "Your father was wicked when that copper told him you'd gone to work. I've never seen him so angry. I wouldn't like to be in your shoes tonight when he gets in – I wouldn't be surprised if he did give you a good hiding. Don't think you're too big, 'cos you're not! You deserve it! Behave like a child, be treated like a child! It might learn you to have a bit more thought for others." She faced me, hands on hips, and leaned forward. "Graeme – how could you be so selfish? Haven't I brought you up better than that? Didn't you give a thought to me? I thought you might have been knocked down, or got into trouble with one of them gangs or summat. I was worried *sick*. And you don't *care*!"

"I *do*," I said, whining and disgusting meself.

"Oh yes, it's very easy to say that, but you hadn't even the decency to let us know, or to come home – just went to work – you make me *sick*! To think after all the trouble I've gone to with you – I *tried* to teach you right from wrong – I *tried* to bring you up properly, and then you go and do a thing like that." She acted very tired and broken-down as she gathered cups from the table. "I give up. You can stop out for a week for me. I shan't care. I know now that I can't expect any consideration or kindness from you." She strolled to the door wearing my bribe, and she added, before going into the kitchen, "You needn't expect any consideration from me either. You needn't come here for your dinners – go to your brother!"

After that she wouldn't speak to me again. She stayed in the kitchen, with nerve-twisting quiet. I couldn't do anything. I felt that until I was forgiven I was a guest in their house and I hadn't any right to leave the room I'd been put in, or disturb them, or touch anything without their permission, not even the right to relax on their furniture. So I perched on the edge of the settee and looked at my hands. All morning and all afternoon. I gnawed at my thumb until it was sore as a boil and bled every time I looked at it. I felt useless, and guilty, and small, and nasty; and she let me feel like that. The cow.

At about six, when I'd been sitting there for seven hours, she came in, switched on the light and drew the curtains. She sat down in Dad's armchair with the paper, but wouldn't switch the telly on because I could watch that too. I was still the unwanted guest, and I was made to feel it.

"Oh, by the way," she said, rustling the paper. "I spoke to your father yesterday dinner-time about that park-job and he didn't seem to mind – but now." She spoiled the casual effect by turning round to see how I'd taken this. I stared vacantly at her, without blinking, because if I blinked, the water would spill out of my eyes, and she'd see it. She looked back to the paper, and I had a small triumph. She hadn't seen the hurt she'd given me.

She stared woodenly at the newsprint, and I knew she was as miserable as I was. I knew she was regretting everything she'd said. I knew that *now*, at that moment, she was weak, and that all I had to do was say, 'I'm sorry' and she'd be all over me, and I could explain, and we could both forgive each other, and then she'd be with me against Dad. Sounds like some soggy film. But I wouldn't, I wouldn't apologise. I couldn't have got the words out anyway. I just could not have said it. So I let it pass, and she grew angry again, because she knew I had. She shook out the newspaper and began to read.

Dad was late. He didn't come in till nearly ten. My heart began to bump when I heard his key in the lock. "Hello, love," Mother said. "All right, are you?"

"Fine," he said, and sat at the table while Mother went for his dinner. I slid him a look. He didn't seem angry, but he was. He ignored me as well, as if I wasn't there. Looked through me, past me. My backbone turned to water and trickled out of my socks.

Mother put Dad's dinner down in front of him, then banged mine down on the other side of the table. She gave me a dirty look, mouth pursed, which meant I was to go and get it.

I stared in front of me and pretended I hadn't noticed. I wanted the dinner, I was hungry – but – I wasn't going to eat it. Partly because it belonged to them, so I had no right to it; and partly just to spite Mother because I knew it made her feel bad.

My Dad finished his dinner and went to sit in his arm-chair. He switched the telly on, but I didn't feel entitled to watch it. Mother sat on a straight-back chair instead of by me. I was like a leper.

At quarter to eleven I got up and left the room, moving stiffly because I expected to be told sharply to sit down. But they didn't say anything. I used the bog and went into my bedroom. I sat on my bed in a heap. I couldn't even stir up any interest in the pornographic magazines under me bed. A horrible thought occurred to me. Tomorrow was my day off, except that I would have to go in for an hour or two to help

Claz wash the floor. I would be here nearly all day.

I was miserable. I got undressed and humped up in bed, fell asleep chewing my thumb.

The next morning I lay in bed for as long as I could stand to before getting up and putting on pants, trousers, socks and shoes. I couldn't hear any sound from the other rooms, the flat might have been empty. Still, I wasn't going out to see in case I bumped into her. Dad would have gone to work hours ago. After a time of lying on the bed, I hung head-downwards and looked underneath for the pile of dirty magazines. They'd gone. I got up and searched in all the drawers. No sign of 'em. Now there was spite. She'd known they were there, because she'd put them into a neat pile every now and then. She'd never said anything, but the first time I put her out she uses it as an excuse.

She suddenly shouted out, "Graeme, if you want summat to eat, you'd better get up!"

"Sod off," I whispered. "You old cow. You bitch." I stayed in my room, sulking. It was unfair. I had a reason for staying out all night, it had been an accident – and there wasn't any way I could have let them know where I was. We don't have a telephone, or bloody homing-pigeons. Two sides could play this game. I could be as awkward as them. No more feeling guilty, no more getting all worked up because they say I'm a naughty boy. To Hell with 'em.

"Graeme, there's tea made if you want any!"

"Shut your face," I whispered, but made no answer that she could hear. I got me transistor-radio an aunt had given me, and switched it on, for the time-checks. When I guessed it was about ten past eleven, I went to the bathroom, washed and combed my hair. Back to the bedroom to put on my shirt and jumper. Mother had hung my jacket up. As I was putting it on in the hallway, she came out of the living-room. "And where d'you think you're going?"

"Work," I said. I zipped up the front of my jacket.

"I want you back here by half past three. Else there'll be

92

trouble."

I felt my mouth and eyes, all stubborn. "What if we'm late finishin'?"

"Oh," she said, "if you're not back by half past three, I shall go down and 'phone the work to see where you are. And you needn't think I won't tell them *why* I want to know."

I didn't answer her, just slammed out of the flat.

I caught the quarter to twelve bus and was at work at twenty past twelve. I didn't answer when Claz called out to me, went straight on upstairs. There was tea in the pot and I poured myself a cup. Drinking it I realised how hungry I was. So I made me some toast on the stove. Two slices. Only made me hungrier.

I went downstairs and started ferrying buckets of hot water into the big tub on wheels. I went along to the rack where the damaged goods are dumped and found a tin of bleach, which I emptied into the water and stirred up with the bottle. Claz went upstairs and fetched the polisher, like a little vacuum-cleaner, that can be used as a dryer as well. He'd be using it as a dryer. "Ready, Graemey? Think we can be done by half one?" This was one of his senile jokes. We never finish before half two.

"I hope not," I said.

"Eh – you hope not?"

"Nothin', Claz," I said, wishing I hadn't spoken.

He came and peered at me. "What's up with thee then?" he asked angrily. "What you so down in the mouth for? What've thee got to be miserable about, at your age?"

I shoved, and got the tub moving, through the swing doors and into the shop. "Forget it, Claz."

"Ooh," he said. "Mardy." He followed me, and we went round to the front of the shop and began. I mopped the floor with the big mop that went with the tub, and Claz plugged in the dryer, and dried it. The Gaffer came round. "You're doin' a good job there. All right are you, Claz?"

"Ar," Claz said, and then the Gaffer said something about

apples and they began to talk. I carried on working, doing my job and Claz's. I wasn't in any hurry, but I was sullen and spiteful, and wanted to point out that I was working and they weren't. I'd finished the aisle and turned the corner before they caught me up.

"He's working well, Clarence," the Gaffer said. "He'll make somebody a good wife one of these days." And when I didn't respond, he came creeping round, trying to see my face. "We've got a long face this morning, Clarence. What's happened, Gray? Lost a fiver and found a penny?"

I wished they'd lay off and stop leading me into the ways of self-pity. "Yeah," I said, and went on grimly working, hoping that they'd go away. I didn't know how much I could take. If they kept on about being miserable and having a long face, I might even cry and the thought of the embarrassment terrified me, it did honest. I squirted the floor with water, and scrubbed it.

"You'm in hurry, Gray," Claz said. "Goin' out after, are you? Got a girlfriend? Takin' her to the back row of the flicks?"

"He don't answer, Clarence," the Gaffer said. "Guilty, I think."

"What's her like, Gray?"

The Gaffer laughed. "Her's either taller than him, or a midget."

"Why don't you laugh, Gray?"

"Oh lay off," I said. The Gaffer stood bolt upright and laughed his head off. I blinked and held my breath. It was a cruel, hard world, and all against me.

They kept plaguing me, asking me about this imaginary girl, saying it was a good job I'd found her because they'd noticed my eyesight had been failing, and did I court her on the side of a hill, or did I take a box with me when I went out with her; could I look her squarely in the knee-caps and swear I'd never been with another girl, and so on; until I was simmering in some state between giggling and tears.

94

Working my way away from them did no good, although I could finish and leave sooner. I mopped the last corner with water and, leaving Claz to dry it, began to push the tub away.

"He's runnin' to her arms, Clarence," the Gaffer said.

"He can't reach that high."

"Well then – he'll just have to be satisfied with what he can reach – eh Gray?" And they both roared with laughter.

But they didn't follow me. I emptied the tub out the back, and took it upstairs in the lift, fetched me jacket and was out.

"Tara, Gray!"

"Tara!"

"Tara," I said as I went outside.

The Church clock said it was half two. I'd missed my 'bus and the next wouldn't be till about ten to three. I went down the road to the caff and spent twenty-one pence on baked beans on toast. Twenty-nine and half pence left. And only Wednesday.

Quarter to three, and I left the caff to walk to the bus-stop. I nagged myself about my cowardice all the way there. Why toe the line and go back? What did it matter? Things weren't going to be sweetness and light anyway.

I wondered if Derek had thought the same thing and decided: To Hell with it.

I decided, to Hell with it, and turned away from the bus-stop, going downhill between ridged factory walls. I thought: all this because I spent a single night out. I thought: if I spend an evening with a friend and come back late it's the same. They don't want me to go out at all. They want me to do only what they say. They want me to be shut up all day at work, and then go home to be shut up there. Claustrophobic, Derek said.

They don't want me to do anything. Don't want me to go out, or drink – Dad'd go beseck if I smoked. Don't even want me to spend me own money. 'You'll spend it in waste, you'll spend it in waste.' So I'm hard up all the time. It's *my* money.

95

I turned off from the street on to a piece of waste-ground, overgrown with stink weed and dog-daisies, marl-hole flowers and Devil's Playthings. There's some of those pretty country names for you. An old factory, half fallen-down and half boarded-up, was one side of the waste's square. I'd meant to get inside this place and have a look round for ages. Now I had the time. There was a window at the back, a big window with grilles and broken glass. A pile of rubble had been made below it. I climbed up and took hold of the grille, hauled myself up. I stood on the narrow ledge, hugging myself to the bars. I could ease through one of the tall spaces, and did, and then, with a bit of manoeuvring, got down till I was hanging at full stretch from the sill, to cut the fall by my own height. I dropped. I only had a foot or two to go.

It was dark inside because all the lower entrances were boarded up, and the windows I'd climbed in through sent their light above my head for the most part. There was rubbish and rubble, chains hanging down, oily ropes making nooses, a stink of cats and damp. Nothing much to hold the interest.

So it started up again. It's my money. I should be able to spend it as I like.

A new and bitter slant on things suddenly occurred to me. This business of saving that Dad was so keen on, putting half my wages away every week, and all of any money that I might get for Christmas and birthdays – it was all a big con. Under cover of guiding my youthful footsteps, he was achieving his own crafty ends – cutting down my freedom by cutting down my spending money.

I didn't altogether like this theory. I didn't like the light it put on my Dad. And I did think that it might owe more to my resentment than it did to Dad. But whichever it was, the more I thought about it, the more sense it made.

Who was it, for instance, that had insisted that I pay all my own expenses from my three pound fifty-five and a half pence, even when Mother had offered to pay my bus-fares?

Who was it had made the family law that I had to ask permission before I could take any money from my own bank-account? Who was it that had insisted that my money should still be banked, with his, in the branch of the Building Society near his work, so that it was right out of my way? And the answer to all these questions – you've guessed it! – the arch-villain of the plot, none other than Richard Bowen, my mother's husband.

I kicked out at a harmless old tin can on the floor, then pelted up a flight of iron stairs. My footsteps clanged and rang from the walls. I stood panting at the top, rubbing my fingers, and feeling the rust-flakes between them from the hand-rail. My Dad's depravity and low cunning shook me.

My mind bounced away from him into a fantastic daydream. I wouldn't suffer under his tyranny any longer. I'd run away, go and live with Derek – hadn't he said I could live there any time I liked? I could live at Bob's and keep all – nearly all – of me wages. Do as I liked.

Dad couldn't stop me. I could just do as I liked.

It was difficult to think of things that I would want to do. At first. Then the ideas started to come. I could go straight out and buy that denim jacket. I could drink, drink, drink – I could invite Vicky out. That was a shaker. Buy her summat expensive – like gin. Or vodka.

She wouldn't come, of course. And I was a minor.

I got more fantastic. I wouldn't stop where Dad could find me. I'd go walkabout, like Derek said. Maybe I could go with him, meet some of these 'funny' people, and then, when I got the hang of it, I could branch out on me own like. Down in London, round Eros with the hippies. Camp out with a tribe of gipsies perhaps – the song, the firelit dances! Freedom. Absolute bloody freedom.

I kicked through the dust and sand on the upper floor. Looked as if it had been a foundry one time. There was a good deal more light up here, because of a door, at least nine feet above the ground, without boarding. Only a little, narrow door. It had been a loading-door. Stuff must have been swung up on a crane. I leaned out and saw, above me, the gantry. I wondered, idly, what stuff had been hoisted up? And who had swung it up, who checked it off? Somebody must have checked it. But whoever they were, they were gone, and I was here.

There must be something – I dunno – inspiring about old places, old rubbish tips. Leaning in the doorway above a jumble of rubbish, I started thinking for the first time. I mean, thinking for myself. I mean, deliberately ignoring what I'd been told by other people, and putting things together for myself. Seeing if I came out to the same answer. And if I didn't, then standing by my own reasoning.

And I mean, using what was in me, what I knew of meself, to try and see what was in others. Going beneath the surface like. Finding summat was round and not just a flat circle.

Dad, I mean Dad. That's what he's always been to me: Dad. You know what I'm gettin' at? A shape, not a person. 'Your Dad says you'll do this, your Dad says you'll do that . . .' Like the giant in a fairy-tale, you know. Big, laughin', a bit frightenin', but not real. But he is real. He's not Dad. He's Richard Bowen, and he's got a life too, had a life, and I'm only incidental to it.

When you come down to it, it's amazing how little I know about my Dad, considering I've lived in the same house for sixteen years. I began to piece together everything I had heard said, been told. His mother died when he was three. He was the youngest but one in a big family. Grandad Bowen never married again. He worked down the Slaughter Pit, Grandad did, and two of his sons were killed down it. It wasn't called the 'Slaughter' for nothing. The Pit closed after the 1926 – that's the General Strike I mean, I need an hour or two to reel off everything I've been told about that – after that, most of the pits round here closed. They were flooded. Grandad Bowen was unemployed for a long time, and his eldest son had to keep the family. And I know that the only sister, me Aunt Gwen, got married and left home. We never hear from her. I've never met her. Get a birthday card occasionally. That was it, all I knew.

But I started to build it up, to see it sort of happening. I began to understand why Dad's always nipping for a quick snog with Mom in the kitchen, and why he's dead set against her working, just wants her at home for when he gets back. And why he comes all over me, especially when he's drunk. There can't have been much love, if that's the word, in Grandad Bowen's house. He wasn't a lovable man when I knew him, and he'd mellowed then, what with stout and senility. But he'd had a life too, in which I'd been less than incidental, and it had been a hard life.

Another thing Grandad Bowen had never had much of was money – now look what Dad had. A comfortable living, a loving wife, a loving son. I mean, speaking conventionally. There's a mouthful. And naturally, having got all that, he was scared of losing it. If Mom was to go to work, she might want to go out with her new friends, hen-parties like. Or shopping with 'em. She wouldn't be there for Dad to come home too then. And if I had more money to spend, I can tell you where I'd be most nights – out with Phil and Steve and them, boozin' and wenchin'. Then it wouldn't be the same for Dad. Me and Mom were important to Richard Bowen.

But we had our lives too.

Except that Mom and Dad weren't exactly incidental to me. Not as yet anyway. Maybe when I'd got what I wanted I could say, 'Oh well, tara for now then,' and stroll off like.

Sixty-four thousand dollar question. What did I want?

My freedom. Very dramatic, Graeme; what does it mean?

Being able to do as I want.

Like Derek?

Yes, like Derek.

My new insight went grinding on, whether I wanted it to or not. I didn't want it to. But it started to add all the things I'd heard, been told, or had picked up about Derek, adding them up and piecing them together into a new Derek, a new Derek and one I didn't much want to see.

Derek had seen a Dad too, a shape blocking his way. Dad hadn't wanted him drinking or staying out late, hadn't liked his friends or his reading, or his opinions. The same old story. So Derek had struck a bold blow for freedom and with one mighty bound he was free. I don't think Derek had ever noticed Richard Bowen.

Derek had got out to Freedom. He'd had a dozen jobs, he'd been a tramp. Busy getting experience, so he said. More than Dad's. Brevitting away, throwing up one job, getting another, searching out 'funny' people; all that experience.

What was he going to do with it? What good was it to him? I ask these questions because I can't think of any answer to 'em. It beats me.

There was just no point to it all. When he'd finished all the job-finding and rigmarole, he hadn't gained anything. Fact is, he was worse off than Dad. He's alone.

I mean, how long can he keep it up? What when he wanted to get married – or live with a girl if that's more his style? Fine while they're both young, I suppose, but not when they need a bit of extra money for coal to keep their old bones warm. And if they have kids, he's going to need a steady income – a job. How's he going to get one with his record? "And where were you working before, Mr. Bowen. I see, and why did you leave? I see. Thank you, Mr. Bowen, goodbye." Great. If he got a job it wouldn't be a very good one – I suppose he could always be a car-worker (by-word for trouble-makers and shoddy, unskilled work. My Dad, for instance, would be ashamed to be called a car-worker. He's skilled).

I suppose he need never get married. Nor stick, even loosely, to one girl. Fine, while he's young – but when he's sixty-four? He's going to be pretty lonely. So what's he going to do?

If he's got any sense, he'll get out. Somewhere along the

line he'll change his mind. Turn back on all he's said. Hypocrite. Work isn't as degrading as being a hypocrite.

I was forced to think that all that talk he'd given me was very thin. And the Derek I saw on the other side of it was unpleasant – a bragging, shouting, swaggering – scared – kid.

So there was only me. There was no Dad I could go and climb up like I did when I was a kid and somethin' on the telly scared me. No Dad, only Richard Bowen, who was as scared as me, scared of having his comfortable life broken up. And there was no big brother to admire for his tallness and beard, his words of wisdom. Just Derek Bowen, and it seemed that he was as daft as I sometimes was. So there was only me, and I felt very lonely.

I leaned my head on my hand, looking down at the marlhole flowers below me. I sighed. I thought, words weren't meant to hurt you. But they do. They're dishonest, words are. They make a disguise for a thing, change the look of it entirely. Then the thing pops through as it really is and half frightens you to death. Or they give you an argument, a real solid argument you can stand on and yell at everybody. Then you think on the words, and the argument's yanked from under your feet and you fall into a deep, dark hole. You get hurt.

Nine feet above the ground this door is, easy. Mother'd have a fit if she was up here, she's scared of heights. She'd have a fit if she knew I was up here. I wondered if she'd phoned Bancroft's yet, but I knew she wouldn't. I knew what Mother would do, and what she wouldn't, what she's like and what not. I was more Thorpe than Bowen. But I didn't care what me mother's real shape was. Let her just be as she'd always been. Helen Thorpe she is, but I don't want to know Helen Thorpe. Just me Mom.

That's a laugh. I want my Mom.

It must have been something to four, because little kids were coming to play on the waste below me. Mom was going to be mad when I got back.

If I went back. But I would. There was nowhere else to go. Blimey, I ought to know better. I used to threaten to run away when I was seven, and Mom used to say, "Here's your bus-fare then." But I wasn't going to spend much longer just decorating Richard Bowen's life. I mean, he hadn't ought to expect me to. I ain't a fairy on a Christmas tree. If I was, I wouldn't be Richard Bowen's son, would I? I'd be some meek and mild little dove with no mind of me own. But I have, even if it hasn't showed very much up till now.

I knew what I wanted. I knew now. First, I want to work in a park, even if that doesn't sound very grand. I want the job *I've* chosen, not the one Dad did. And secondly, I want somebody who'll look up to me and admire me: me, ar, me – little diddy Graeme Bowen. I've always wanted that. I've always worked hard, trying to get Vicky, for instance, to admire me, but she doesn't. That's what I wanted above everything else. Admiration.

And I decided I was going to get it. Richard Bowen wasn't going to stop me, and Derek Bowen wasn't going to fool me.

Mother had told me to be back by half three, but it was going to be more like half four. Well, that was it. They weren't going to lay down these laws for me any more. Bloody hell, I was sixteen, not six. I didn't think Mother would make any row about my being late. Fact is, I knew she wouldn't.

And the job at Bancroft's was going. I was packing it in. Maybe not with fireworks and public speeches – but I wasn't going to be around to take that exam. Then we'd see about a park job.

I wondered what time it was. There would be a bus at quarter to four. The drop at my feet. It would terrify Mother. I suddenly gave a yodelling Tarzan yell, that stunned all the little kids below, and leapt straight out.

The air rushed past me and I shut my eyes. I didn't know how I landed. I don't know how I landed, except that I was breathless, bruised, but all in one piece. I stood up, thinking:

What a bloody stupid thing to do, and laughing like a drain. All these little kids stood round with their thumbs in their mouths and staring eyes. They hadn't even seen me up there, let alone expected me to drop on 'em from a great height. I ran to catch my 'bus.

As soon as I opened our door and went into the hall, I realised that whatever airy thoughts I'd had, things at home hadn't changed. The air closed round me. I hung my coat in the hall and went straight to my bedroom. I heard Mother, in the hall, say, "Graeme?" But she must have seen my coat, because she went back into the living-room, and there was quiet.

In my room I crooned over my cactus, and tried again to warm me jumping-beans into life. I searched every cupboard and drawer for my smutty magazines, but Mom had taken them all right. That was one thing I'd never guessed she'd do. It was one of the things that would make her Helen Thorpe, if I cared to delve about there, but I didn't. I was talking to the cactus again, urging her on, when the door slammed back against the wall and Dad was there. He made a sharp movement of his hand to show that I should go to him. I stood up slowly.

"Out!" he said. "Come on. You needn't think you're going to sulk in there, putting your Mother in the wrong. Move!"

You can't lay down laws for Graeme any more. But I went out past him and into the living-room. Now he'd started talking to me again, it'd soon be over.

I sat down on the edge of the settee, and Mother brought two dinners in. "Your dinner's here, Graeme."

I didn't answer, and Dad shouted, "Hey! You're being spoken to! Your mother says your dinner's here!"

I looked away as if I hadn't heard.

"Let him get on with it," Dad said.

Mother went to make the tea. A couple of minutes passed, and then Dad snapped, "Aren't you going to come and eat this dinner?" I could hear Richard Bowen, afraid that his life was being disturbed.

"No," I said. A bit cruel, I think.

"Right," Dad said. "It won't go to waste. I can eat it. You'll get nothing else in this house." Threats, threats, empty threats.

Mother came back with the stewed tea. I heard it splashing into cups. "I've poured you one, Graeme."

"Thanks," I said flatly, but didn't go to get it.

Dad finished his dinner and slowly slurped a cup of tea. He came and sat down heavily in his armchair, was quiet for a moment, and then pronounced, "I'm ashamed of you, young man."

And that went straight through and got me where I lived. Richard Bowen vanished and there was Dad again. I was guilty as Hell because he was ashamed of me. He was right and I was wrong. I should never have stayed out all night, I should never have let myself get mixed up and caught up. . . . I should have come home. Lamb to the fold and all that.

He stood up and cleared his throat, and shuffled on the hearth, standing over me like a judge, while I sat on the settee and hung my head. "I thought −" he began. "I thought −" He stopped and coughed. "This has got to be said," he told himself, and started again from the beginning. "I thought that I had a son who was intelligent, responsible and − adult. But I find I was mistaken. I find you go off without a word to us, spend the night away from home with us not knowing where you are − and *then* − and then − you *don't* come home in the morning − you go to work as if nothing had happened! Leave us to go on worrying!" He coughed and rubbed at one eye. I thought: I know, I know, I know what I did! There's no need to tell me again. It seemed hopeless to try and explain how I'd meant to come home but never got around to it − and how I'd meant to go home but had to go to work − it was a weak excuse. He'd never believe. And if I told him the truth − that I'd meant to come home Tuesday morning, but had been afraid to, he'd want to know what I was afraid of, and I couldn't tell him. I didn't really know.

He started up again, "I don't want to lose my temper. I think that what you did Monday was irresponsible in the extreme —"

"I meant to come on Tues —" I'd meant to say it loud, but it stayed a whisper in my throat.

"What? *What?*"

"I meant to come Tuesday, but I was late and I had to go to work," I said miserably. It seemed an age before I'd finished, and my face got hotter with every word. He thought it over. It was one of his maxims that a man who never shirked his work was a good man. But in the end he found a way round it.

"That hardly improves matters, does it? It makes me think that you think more of work than of me and your mother. You were irresponsible to us. You went with your brother and that gang of yobbos he lives with?"

I nodded.

"I don't like saying that you can't see your brother — after all, he *is* your brother — I'd like to see him — *but* — but I'd prefer you not to mix with him and his mates. Lay-abouts. I forbid you to go there again. Understand? I forbid you."

I didn't say anything, I didn't nod. I didn't even particularly *want* to go and see Derek again, but I would be. Because Dad said I couldn't. He couldn't make laws for me any more. I couldn't let him, could I? Or he'd make a thingy, a hypocrite out of me. I'd go under.

"I don't want you going the same way as him," Dad said. He seemed to be hinting at dark things. "You don't go there again. Do you hear?"

"I hear," I said.

"Right," he said. "Now that's understood." He coughed and stood uncomfortably in front of the electric fire. "Just so long as that's understood." He turned away to the mantelpiece, and I thought he'd finished, but he turned round again and said, "I may as well settle this other matter while I'm on." My ears pricked up. "Your mother tells me that you want to change your job, want to leave Bancroft's. When she told me I thought –"

We didn't get to hear what he'd thought. He stopped and I held my breath.

"But now – I don't think you're old enough to make that decision. I don't think you've shown the responsibility – you've got a good job now. As a manager you could make fifty pound a week. And it's not a dead end job. It's not a job you go into and then stop thinking about everything but what's in your wage-packet and how much is a pint of beer. I'd hate to see you in a job like that. In this job you ain't stopped learnin', you'll get on and you never will stop learnin'. Now, you'd have to do a lot of thinking before you throw up a job like that – right-minded thinkin'. It's a responsible decision. It could affect your whole life." He paused impressively. "I think you've proved that you haven't got the responsibility – you haven't got the experience of life. You don't know you'm born yet. You get this idea you'd like to be a gardener – a gardener, for God's sake. If they make twenty pound a week it's as much as they do – that's nothing these days. You get some hare-brained idea about bein' a gardener and straight away you want to give up this good job you've got. You've give it no more thought than you would to – to buyin' one of your blasted records, all drone and noise. Inside a week you'd be fed up of bein' out in the rain or bein' give all the dirty jobs to do. I think it's my duty to stop you." He nodded several times. "My duty." Heavy sigh. "I suppose when you're eighteen you'll do as you like, and if you still think the same way, I promise I won't say anything." Very big of him. He turned to Mother and said, "Worst thing they ever did, lowering the age to eighteen. Kids ain't fit to cross the road by theirselves at eighteen. I wasn't."

He still stood on the hearth as if expecting some comment from me, but there didn't seem to be anything that I could say. He'd worked it all out for me. And I couldn't say anything about my determination *not* to go on the way he'd laid out.

He must have decided that enough had been said, he had spoken and I had understood, because he clapped his hands and rubbed them together with great relief. "Aren't you going to eat that dinner?"

"It's cold now," Mother said, who had been listening from the side-lines, agreeing, or at least keeping her opinions to herself.

I could see it was my cue to apologise. I didn't feel apologetic at all, but it would make living easier. Anything for a quiet life. "I didn't mean not to come home. They kept saying they'd give me a lift and it like snowballed. I didn't mean to worry you."

"Ar," Dad said, on a low rumble, but I think he guessed about the booze. Maybe that's why he was so keen on my not going there again.

"An' I would have come back Tuesday mornin', but I had to go to work."

"Ar," Dad said. "I see that, but you should have come back just the same. You could have gone to work in the afternoon."

There was an itchy silence until Dad bent down and switched on the telly. The programme flickered up, music began and everyone seemed to jump and come to life again. "I could do you egg on toast," Mom said. "That all right?"

"Please."

"I'll make a fresh pot of tea while I'm on." She went into the kitchen to kill the fatted egg.

Dad crashed down by me on the settee, and all the springs groaned. He put his arm along the back, and pulled a hair from the top of my head. Ouch. "Mah favourite son," he said. He put his arm around my neck and tightened it against me throat. "But if you do anythin' like that again, I'm warnin' you, you can get your bones ready." Then he

107

dragged my head down against his chest, scrubbed my hair into knots, and laughed.

Mother came in with a fresh bottle of milk and caught sight of herself in the mirror. She prinked, lifting her hair at the back and fingering the shell necklace. She turned at the noise we were making and looked down. I was kicking at the arm of the settee, trying, without any success at all, to get Dad's arm from around me neck. Dad was sweaty-faced, laughing all over his mush. "What are you two playin' at? Like two saft school-kids."

All was forgiven.

But not bloody well forgotten.

As I told my cactus that night, "I was right, you know. Dad just don't want me to have any freedom. He thinks I can't look after meself. Well, I can. I ain't just bein' saft, wanting to be a gardener, I ain't. I don't *like* the job I've got. What's the good of livin' if you spend it doin' what somebody else wants you to do instead of summat you like? Derek made that much sense anyway. And what's the good of workin' all week if you can't spend the money the way you want? I wouldn't mind givin' Mom four quid – I wouldn't mind givin' her five if I could do as I liked with the rest."

I stood up and pulled off my jumper. Unbuttoning my shirt, I turned on the cactus, pointing at it for effect. "An' he says, in two years' time I can do as I like, but that's two years gone and wasted! I'll never have that two years again." I told the cactus, "It's all right for him! It ain't his life!"

I got into bed and sat up, hugging my knees. Two more years stuck in that job. Two years of stacking soap-powders. Two years of yawning. I couldn't stand it.

I could push, I could insist, I could hand in my notice – if I really wanted the fat in the fire. He'd raise Cain.

What I needed was a way to get out of Bancroft's without stirring the muck up too much.

Too much to hope for.

I flopped back on to my pillow, and the bump must have

activated me brain, because a second later I was sitting slowly up, like Frankenstein's monster coming to life. I could see the furry bump of my cactus in the dark. "I *know*," I said to her.

5

It was the tea-break. I'm not on first tea-break with Vicky and Brenda and them. I'm on second with Claz, and Harry the butcher, and Perce, the surly old beggar, and Mrs. Harris, and Barb off the wines – all the old uns. So I'm out of it. I sit by Claz, 'cos he's me mate, but he only stuffs his face with sausage sandwiches and moans about the price of cabbage, and the weather. Perce boasts about how his wife nags him, and Harry talks about how he took his missis out, and they danced the fox-trot. The women have grisly conversations about babies being born that put me right off the idea of being born, or getting anybody else born, when I listen. There's none of it anythin' to do with me, an' if I do try to join in, they only laugh at me and take the mick. Make out I don't know what I'm talking about. So I usually just sit with the chair tipped back on two legs, drink me tea, and look at the patterns in the top of the table. Even that don't stop 'em plaguing me when they've got nothing else to talk about. That's the trouble with being the youngest.

This tea-break I was trying to work something out. If you've got a good record of two years' satisfactory work, what's the quickest and surest way of getting the sack?

I can tell you. Be caught stealing. But I didn't want to end up in a Borstal.

Apart from stealing, the firm'd take a lot from me before

110

they fired me. It would be as quick to give notice. You have to give a month's notice at Bancroft's. Still, that would be my doing. If I was sacked, it would be more on the firm's side.

"Graeme's quiet."

"Uh?" I said. "Somebody speak to me?"

"You're quiet," Barb said.

They were all watching me, must have been for ages. Claz sniggered. "Thinkin' about your girl-friend, ain't you, Gramey?"

"Have you got a girl-friend, Graeme?" Barb asked, and all the women sort of brightened up and got interested.

"I'm his girl-friend," Mrs. Harris said. "Ain't I, Gray?"

"Yeah, sure," I said, thinking that this might turn the teasing on to her more than me.

"He's my young man," Mrs. Harris said, leering.

"You should find yourself a nice girl," Barb said, after the slight giggle had died down. She said this as if passing on a real pearl of wisdom like.

"He won't need to look," Mrs. Harris said. "Good-looking young lad like him, all the girls'll come runnin'." She rolled her eyes and winked. "If I was a couple of years younger, I'd lift up me skirts an' run too."

"You'd need to be more than a couple of years younger," Harry said, laughing, and Mrs. Harris said, "Oh you," and thumped him. Everybody laughed louder until that joke was finished, and then they turned on me again, when I'd been hoping they'd forgotten me.

"I know he's got an admirer," Mrs. Harris said, as my face got hot. "A secret admirer. Watches him from afar, she does, with big wide eyes, and when he's not about she comes creeping up to me and says, 'Mrs. Harris, is Graeme here today?'"

"Aahh," Barb said.

"Innit sweet?" Jen asked.

They really make me sick. I was very red by now and sat looking at my cup, pretending I hadn't heard.

111

"Who's this then, Reet?" Harry asked.

"Ah, that would be telling." But when she got up to pour herself another cup of tea she came back to the table past him, bent and whispered in his ear. His red face lit up. "Oh, you'm on to a good thing there, Gray. Pretty little thing." He gave me thumbs up. "Get in there, lad." Claz sniggered.

"I've got better things to think about than girls," I said angrily, which was far from the truth.

"Ooh – hark at him," Barb hooted.

"He's goin' to sail round the world," Harry said.

"You'm thinkin' of your exam, ain't you, Gray?" Jen said, sticking up for me. "He's got to work hard to pass it. So you leave him alone."

I wasn't thinking of anything of the kind. Fact is, I stopped doing the lessons, I was so determined to get out of here before the exam came up. I didn't know how long it would be before they notified the Gaffer about me not sending the lessons back.

I said, "If you was very rude to a customer, would you get the sack?"

They all stopped talking for a minute. Claz snorted, "What you want to know that for?"

"I just wondered."

"Well, wonder about summat else."

"I suppose it depends on how rude you was," Harry said.

Jen was authoritative. "No, you wouldn't. Not just for bein' rude. I mean, some folk can be that awkward – you wouldn't be human if you didn't lose your temper sometimes."

"Have you been being rude to the customers then, Graeme?" Mrs. Harris asked sternly.

"No! No, 'course not."

"It sounds like it to me."

"Well, I haven't. What if you went on bein' rude, Jen?"

"I suppose they'd sack you if they had enough complaints," she said.

112

"I think he is up to no good," Mrs. Harris said, nodding, folding and unfolding her double chins.

I looked at my watch. "I'd better go."

"You've no need to go yet," Claz snapped. "Stop for another five."

"I'm goin'." I swilled my cup at the sink. "Please yourself," Claz said, as I went out.

It seemed the answer was about a week of concentrated bad behaviour. Not a week – three days, if I could do it. I was going to be busy. And unpopular.

But for all that, starting from now, I was going to be as rude, as unhelpful, as idle and as generally useless as I knew how to be.

I didn't like it. It makes you a bit nervous, to deliberately – and I didn't fancy being unhelpful to Mrs. Harris, and Claz, who's my mate.

But it was no good backing out because of things like that. I saw, as I came down the stairs, that there was some baling badly needed. The back was knee-deep in cardboard. So I left it.

I went into the shop and poked about for something to do, just to while away the time. I was strolling down the aisle between the fridges when this thin woman with glasses stopped me. "Is there any of that margarine that was special, cheap, last week?"

"What marg was that? Our brand, super-soft was it?" I asked, out of habit.

"Well, it was in a tub – a yellow one I think."

I remembered my role. "I don't know, don't care," I said, and marched briskly off. Guilt set in sharply. Shouldn't have done that, Graeme. That woman'd done nothin' to you. But I worked hard at curing this weakness. She's incidental to you, Graeme, that woman. You'm workin' to an end. You can't afford to be sentimental.

I got my second chance at three o'clock when I was going up to my tea. Claz was busy on his counter and he wanted his tea too. "Gramey – give us hand, will you?"

Well – I would have helped – Claz's my mate – but – "No. I'm goin' for me break," I said.

I went slow up the stairs. It wasn't fair on Claz. He's always been good to me and it was a nice way to pay him back. It was worse because Claz never said anything about it.

I worked hard at it though, and I really got into the swing of it after a while, what with being determined to get meself sacked. I was rude to the customers with a – a dedication that even shook me: Never a blush or a blink. I didn't know I had it in me. I mean, some of them women – especially the old uns – they'm frightenin'.

And then I shirked and skived. I didn't do the baling until the Gaffer searched me out and told me to, but the next day, when he told me to go and help Perce on the Cooked Meats, I went and wasted time on the little bit of baling there was to do, because Perce's a surly old beggar and I didn't want to work under him.

The way you bale is like this: you get a baler, and you break down all the boxes and you throw 'em into the baler. Trays and bits of cardboard like that you just put in. All the rubbish you throw into the yard and set fire to.

Now, when the baler's full, you crank the handle, and that brings down a plate that presses all the cardboard together tight. When you've cranked it down as far as it will go, you fix the handle to hold it down, but you have to watch it, because sometimes the catch don't lock properly and then the handle flies up and cuts your face open. It's laid my head open once, and nearly had me eye out, and give me more bruises than I can remember. Now I lean away from it, very awkward.

But, if you've got it locked, then you get these things like a hook and eye. There's a long loop of metal, that you double the baling-string through, and there's these two slits down the front and back of the baler, and you push the loop and the string through one of these slits. It's a tight fit, so you have to

114

kick it in, or get the shovel and hammer it in. Then you go round the back of the baler, with this long, thin hook, and you poke it into the slits and fish around until you get hold of the string in the loop. Then you can pull it through. You do this top and bottom, both sides, and then you can tie the cardboard up really tight. Then you just open the baler and take out one neat bale. I think there must be an easier way.

But you'll understand when I say I was hammering the loop into the bottom of the baler, with the shovel, when I heard the Gaffer calling me. The door was open, the loading-door, so I nipped out, jumped off the loading-step, and ran around behind the wall.

I heard the Gaffer say, "Well, where is he, Clarence? Did you light this fire?"

Claz must have denied it, because the Gaffer yelled again, "Graeme!"

Pressed against the wall, only a few feet from them, I came over all giggly and had to stick my thumb in my mouth to stop it.

"Well, where is he?" the Gaffer asked again, and I heard the door slide back. I hoped they hadn't locked it.

I let a few minutes pass before going back. Claz must have shut the door, because it wasn't locked. The Gaffer would have locked it, that's a sure bet. To stop 'reptiles' getting in — that's what he calls the reps from the different firms. I eased it back and slipped inside. I began to hammer the loop in again, very industriously. To tell the truth, I was very nervous about what the Gaffer would say. I was still hammering when he came downstairs.

"Gray! Gray, where have you been?"

I sat back on my heels and looked up at him. "Eh?"

"I've been looking for you high and low. Couldn't find you anywhere. Where've you been?"

"When?" I said.

"Just!"

"I was here," I said, "an' in the yard burnin' rubbish."

115

He began to get annoyed. "You weren't. We couldn't find you."

"Ah well – I did go for a quick breather round the park – that's probably where I was." Oh Christ, I thought, with a queer mixture of fear and excitement, that's done it! He was wicked as a wasp.

"You went for a walk round the park."

"That's right," I said, as coolly as I could.

"What d'you think this is – a holiday camp? – And what were you doing here? I thought I told you to go on the Cooked Meats?"

I had to cough before I could answer. Gaffer-baiting's a game that stirs up the emotions a bit. He was a sight bigger bloke than me an' all, and he was getting very mad. "I didn't feel like it yet. I was goin' to go later."

He come towards me very fast, and I jumped up and back, because it looked as if he was going to relieve his feelings by kicking me feet from under me. But he only yelled, "Well, get over there *now*, and hurry up!"

Summat being the better part of valour, and all that, I dropped the loop and went. I skidded round behind the Cooked Meats and said, "I'm here."

Perce gave me the corner of an evil eye. "When I've got a chance I'll hang the flags out."

I got me own back by mauling the cheese and bacon that I served, and weighing the butter wrong; charging the wrong prices and generally messing things up. Every time I allowed meself to think, even for a glimpse, of the bawling-out that was coming to me for all this, me innards drew up on themselves. But I wouldn't think of it and kept grimly on. The bawling-out wouldn't last for ever and then came the rest of my life. I hoped I could get the bawling-out over and done with soon.

But Friday passed, and Saturday. I'd hoped to be finished by then but no such luck. Things were building up. The air between me and the Gaffer fairly crackled every time he looked at me. Even Claz was short. I got nothing but filthy looks from Perce.

Mrs. Harris wasn't so retiring, not by half. I was passing the fruit counter at a slack time, about two o'clock on the Saturday, when she said, "Graeme – come here, come on."

I went over to her. She had her arms folded and a sour face. "What have I done *now*?" I asked, joking.

She took the wind out of my sails a bit. "That's just it," she said. "Why're you being such a naughty boy?"

My face turned hot. Discovered! I thought, Betrayed! "How'd you mean?" I said, pretending that I wasn't looking as guilty as Hell.

"You know very well what I mean, my young sprig o' the green," she said severely, staring at me.

I shuffled uneasily, and tried to bluff. "No I don't – I mean – how – I haven't done owt!"

"Oh – h – he hasn't done anything." After saying this, she let the minutes tick away until I looked nervously over my shoulder, half expecting to find the Bogey-Man there, ready to stuff me into his sack and race off. "All this week you've been playing up. And what's this about *refusing* to help Mr. Pritchard when I was on me tea-break and he'd a lot to serve?"

I couldn't say anything to this, and besides, it hadn't been right to leave old Claz in it up to his ears. I had no defence at all. I looked down at me feet and sort of shrugged and swayed on one leg.

"You need look ashamed of yourself," Mrs. Harris said.

"Oh come on, Mrs. Reet," I said, pleading for forgiveness.

"Oh no, *oh* no, don't you 'Mrs. Reet' me. You want to pull your socks up, my lad. We've all got to do work we don't like, we just have to learn to put up with it. And you'll have to learn to put up with it."

I pulled a sulky face and said, "I don't see why I should put up with it . . ."

"Because you'll get a thick ear otherwise, my darling, and

117

I'll be the one to give it you!"

I detected a weakening in this threat and looked up with a grin. "Oh yeah? Like to take your jacket off and step into the yard?"

"Oooh," she said. "I could gobble you up in two mouthfuls and spit out the bones!"

"You sound like a bloody owl!"

"You shouldn't swear at your age, it's not right. Here," she said, "you look a scribe." She whipped a comb out of her breast-pocket – it's a breast-and-a-half-pocket – and said, "Come here, you scribe." She combed my hair, turning me this way and that with a podgy warm hand on my shoulder. She combed my fringe right down and it covered my eyes, so she put it to one side. "When Robert was alive I always combed his hair for him. He could never get the parting right."

"No," I agreed, wincing patiently as she raked the comb through my scalp.

"There." She pulled the shoulders of my overall square, smoothed my lapels, perfected the knot of my tie. "You might wash your face when you've got the time, it's grubby."

"I might," I said. She lifted up my hair as an afterthought, turned me round and inspected my neck and ears. "You'll do. My boys would never have washed if I didn't check on them. Not even when they were great big lads."

"Can I go now?" I asked.

"I'll let you."

I nipped into the back, out of her sight, and rubbed my hair scruffy again, and shrugged me overall comfortable and untidy. The Gaffer peered at me from his office, and I belted up the stairs as if I had something to do. I hadn't.

I skived hard all that day until half-past five, but it didn't get me the sack, so it all dragged on to the next week. Monday I didn't do the stock-cards, I baled instead; I'd mislaid an invoice, and that had everybody in a tizz-wazz; I'd given Ian a price three pence too cheap to put on the sauces,

118

and those sauces had sold well Saturday. It was a good day and a bad day, depending on how you looked at it. At least I knew I was getting up the Gaffer's nostrils.

But it was all getting me down. I kept on with it because it seemed too late to turn back, but I was miserable, what with feeling guilty about Claz and Mrs. Harris, and the others looking down their noses at me. And this feeling of doom drawing ever nearer, because I knew I was going to get a real bawling-out from the Gaffer.

Mother asked if I was feeling well. She's like that, Mother. I told her I was fine, which I was, just nervous, that's all. My cactus-flower opened, but I couldn't get any pleasure from it, and me Mom still hadn't returned me pornographic magazines, that great stimulant. And I couldn't very well ask her where they were. She wasn't supposed to know anything about them.

Another week drew out, and I began to feel that the others at work were really starting to hate me. They suffered me and I just suffered. They cut me short if I talked, turned their backs on me, didn't say hello or 'All right?' and normally they never stop asking if you're all right. Sometimes I'd think maybe it was all my imagination, but it wasn't. I was getting myself disliked in no uncertain way. It made me so miserable I began to think about giving up and returning to my former well-behaved ways – and that made me even more miserable –

My resolve, as they say, was strengthened on Saturday. I'd been helping Perce on the Cooked Meats. He hadn't wanted me helping him, and I hadn't wanted to help, so things had been humming all morning. About dinner-time I took a skip out. It had been used to bring some sides of bacon over from the loading-door, and it was in the way, so Perce said take it in the back. I think he wanted to get rid of me. I gave it a push, jumped aboard and rode it across the shop with a lot of noise.

I hopped off at the biscuit-fixture because I saw Eileen, the little Saturday girl, in a bit of an affray with an ugly customer. I strolled over. "What's up?" I said.

Eileen just turned and looked at me with big brown eyes. Her face was blank and calm, like a little china doll's, but her eyes were all confused and worried. "What what what *what*?" I said, and grinned at her.

She didn't answer, but the customer shoved his oar in. I knew him well. He comes in every week, with his little purse, so tiny he can barely get his finger and thumb into it, his prissy mouth, his tip-toeing walk and his finicky ways. He's got to have everything just so, bags folded neatly, goods weighed to the quarter-ounce, instant, slave-type service. He pushed a packet under my nose. "These biscuits," he said.

I backed off and looked them over. "Yes," I said. "Cheese Puffs. Very nice they are. What's your complaint?"

"They've gone up four pence – *four pence* since last week!"

"Get on to Head Office, don't come to me, butty."

He looked really shocked for a minute. As if I'd dropped down on hands and knees and bit him in the leg. Honest, some of the folk who come in – they expect you to take anything they dish out, and never give a murmur.

"I want to see the manager!" he said at last.

My wit was sharpened by my dislike of him, and Eileen being there. "Then go to your optician."

He was lost for words again. He looked confused, and I swelled. He gabbled, "I *insist* that you fetch the manager – I insist, young man – and I shall mention your extremely ignorant manners to him."

"You do that," I said. "Be sure you do that."

After a second, he demanded, "Are you going to fetch the manager?" He almost stamped his little foot.

"No," I said.

Deadlock. He looked round, hoping the Gaffer would materialise like a genie. He drew himself up. "Then I shall – "
We never knew what he would. He turned round and tiptoed off. To find the Gaffer I suppose. I didn't care. I waved him

off like something out of Monty Python. Good riddance. Off he went clutching his cheese puffs, all stiff and livid.

"Hope he breaks his neck," I said, but didn't expect any answer from Eileen, she's too shy. As I turned away I caught sight of her face – and there was enough admiration there to send me sailing right up into the clouds. She thought I was a big man, reckless and swash-buckling, debonair: James Bond and John Wayne all rolled into one, just because I'd lipped that beggar. I felt me back stiffen with pride, and me head went up, me hair rose like a lion's mane. "'Bout time somebody told that one," I said, "and it takes me to do it. I don't stand for no shovin' around."

She stared at me, all brown-eyed and her little mouth open. "Won't you be in trouble?" she whispered.

"What? From the Gaffer? Huh – he don't worry me – I don't care what he says. He says owt to me, I shall tell *him* an' all."

"He might sack you."

"Don't care if he does," I said lightly. "Get another job, don't matter to me." And I leapt on to me chariot, and roared off, crashing through the double doors. I didn't look round, but I prickled all over with the knowledge that big brown eyes were watching me. Female admiration – it don't half make your part - heart! - *heart* beat. It really does.

While I was steering the skip into place beside the lift, the Gaffer came in from the shop. He gave me a quick glance. "Perce's fixture could do with a wipe-down, the walls and all. You can get on and do it now."

I was still above myself, high on admiration. I looked at my watch. "I was on last night, I knock off at one today. It's quarter past twelve now."

The Gaffer came to an abrupt halt, and gave me a dirty look. He said, "Then go and make a start – now."

I went out into the shop, and to Claz and Mrs. Harris on the fruit counter. "D'you want your fixture washed down, Claz – ah, I'll rephrase that – do you want the walls and

121

shelves washed?"

He froze, and watched me from his little bright eyes. He made a grumbling noise. "What? Wash down? What's this?"

"The Gaffer says I've got to wash the Cooked Meats down, and I thought I may as well do the Fruit as well."

"Ar, I suppose. Ar, go on then."

"I'll do you first then," I said, and went and got a bucket of hot water and a cloth, and a damaged box of soap-powder. And washing the Fruit took so long that I never got around to the Cooked Meats, which needed it.

But still I didn't get the sack. It all limped on until the next Monday. I went into work as tight-wound as a watch-spring. I'd waited and waited for the big yell, but nothing happened, and I just couldn't stand it any longer. Like waiting for the other shoe to drop, if you know that joke. I gave up. The day dragged out and I did everything I was told, and some things I wasn't – I did me job, though wearily. I was broken, as they say. They'd tamed me.

About half three I was sitting on a skip in the biscuit-room, filling in a stock-card and waiting to be called to help with the delivery. All of a sudden the smug, supermarket music cut off, and the Gaffer's voice said, "Mr. Bowen to the office, *please*."

I jumped up off the skip, stiff and alive with delight. This is it! I thought. He's had enough. The sack! I ran to the door, but stopped with a jerk as I thought of the next few minutes. This was also the big yell, the embarrassing, agonising lecture. Me thumb went into me mouth and I bit it. I hoped he wouldn't get too mad.

But what the hell, Graeme! Shout right back!

Yeah – but he was right. I mean, there was nobody who deserved the sack like me – I'd been working on it.

Go on, coward, get it over with.

I was going to go, but I thought: Hang on a bit. Make it good. Let him call again.

122

Or, in other words, put it off a bit. Go a bit later. Not yet.

Either way, I sat on the skip and waited. I got right worked up, sniggering to meself like an idiot and biting me thumb, and saying, "Hey, hey, hey – in a bit though!" I felt all shaky and breathless with excitement, and when the Gaffer's voice came, "Mr. Bowen!" I got up and raced down the stairs for all that I was worth.

But downstairs, though I bubbled like a kettle inside, I was a good deal more casual. I trotted carelessly up the office steps. "You call me, Gaffer?"

He glared. "I did. Twice."

"Sorry. I didn't hear you."

He doubted this, but couldn't prove I had. "Come on in – and shut the door. I've got summat to say to you."

Great, I thought, great! I've got the sack! I could feel a grin stretching my face and fought to straighten it out. I shut the door and sat down on the spare stool, one leg under me, and the other hooked round the stool's stem. The Gaffer raised an eyebrow. "Sit down, why don't you?" My grin burst loose again, and I found I was biting my thumb. I snatched it out of my mouth and pressed both hands down on the seat of the stool, raising myself up. I was – elated. I was sure of what he was going to say. I was sacked.

He shuffled some papers in his hands, price-lists, trying to square them off. He said, "That frozen-food – faggots – come in Friday. You checked the invoices, didn't you?"

"Yeah," I said.

"Where are they?"

"What? The invoices?"

"What else?" he snapped.

"I dunno," I said. The best of it was, I didn't. As far as I could remember I'd dealt with the faggots in a way that couldn't be faulted. I felt in the pockets of my overall, but the invoices weren't there. "I don't know, Gaffer. Shall I go and look – "

"Hang on. Sit down. I've had Brenda lookin' in the fridge

123

and all over the place. We can't find them. You haven't got 'em on you?"

"No, Gaffer."

He sighed and sat staring at the papers in his hands. At last he said, "Your work's been very bad just lately."

"Yes, Gaffer," I said happily.

"What d'you mean – yes?"

"Ah –" I said, and looked down.

"I've had more complaints about you this past week or two – bein' rude – and unhelpful. Not just from the custo-mers either. From the staff, some of it." He stared moodily out of his office window at the shoppers in the aisles below. I squirmed at the thought of my mates on the staff being so riled with me that they'd complained to the Gaffer. He started up again suddenly, "You've been late every mornin' – dinner-time too. Three times I've caught you slyin' off early – and skivin'. Walking round the park. What's come over you? You hadn't used to behave like this. What are you play-ing at? Are you trying to get the sack?"

I opened my mouth, but then thought better of it. He was watching my face very hard and I started to get red. "No," I mumbled.

"You're going the right way about it! Your conduct this late week has been – appalling. No other word for it. Ter-rible. I should fire you – you would have been at any other place before now – but I can't understand it." He shook his head sadly.

A dart of alarm shot into me. It seemed he wasn't con-vinced. I'd underestimated how well I'd become fitted in with the rest of the staff over two years – Claz, Mrs. Harris – even Perce. They made excuses for me. I could just see Mrs. Harris telling everybody how awkward I'd become, and then turning round as soon as somebody agreed with her, and explaining why I was, poor little sod.

"You've always done good work before. I thought you were a bright lad. Reliable. I've been able to tell you to do a

124

thing, and you've got it done without running to me every five minutes like Claz does. And you'd do things off your own bat – I'd go to do 'em and find 'em already done. You've took work off my back, and you could be trusted to get on with the job and do it well, so I know I don't have to go and check it. Initiative – that's why I recommended you for the Managerial Course. What's come over you?"

"Nothin'," I said, embarrassed by this back-handed praise.

He got a bit annoyed. "There must be some reason why, all of a sudden, you can't be trusted to do anything right. Or even trusted to do what you've been told to do!"

"No reason," I said, and then decided to convince him once and for all that there was no excuse for me. "I'm fed up, that's all. I couldn't be bothered to do 'em right – or be polite – or anythin'."

He stared out of the office window and breathed a bit heavy. Brenda came in for a new price-tape, and he wouldn't say anything while she was there, so he had time to recover himself.

"Well, you'd better buck up and get bothered, young man." He sucked at his teeth a while. "I think you've been – very rude, but that's beside the point." Another long pause. "Your work's been bad but only in the past week or so. We all get fed up sometimes and you've always given satisfaction before. So I'm going to let you off this time. . . ."

Oh bloody hell, what's the use? Everything's against you, why not just give up? He went on talking but I was sort of hanging in shock, and I didn't hear him.

"What's the matter, Gray?"

I drew in a long breath that juddered, and my mouth pulled awkward, for all my efforts to stop it. "Nothin'!"

"What you pullin' faces for, Gray? Are you all right?"

I got up fast. "I'm all right, yes, fine!" I was cussin' and callin' meself everything. I turned for the door but couldn't find the handle. And then a noise found its way out of my

mouth, so queer that even I could hardly recognise it. "Gray
– what's up?"

"Nothin', there's nothin' wrong, there's nothin'!" I felt
half-throttled. I was terrified that I might start properly to
cry.

The Gaffer put one hand against the door and leaned on it.
He was worried. He thought I was going to throw an epi-
leptic fit. "Gray – sit down – what's up? What you – what's
the matter, for God's sake?"

"Nothin'," I said furiously, "I keep tellin' you – " After
that he leaned against the door while I snivelled, choked and
hiccupped. I don't know who was madder, him or me, but I
couldn't do anything, not even stop whining. I felt like biting
off my own hands. If I'd been a cat, I'd have looked like a por-
cupine. Somebody rattled at the handle, but with the Gaffer
leaning on it, it was as good as locked.

Still, at the thought of somebody else coming in as well, I
sniffed, gulped and took another shaky breath. I thought I'd
beaten it. Bitterly ashamed, I wiped my face dry with me
overall cuff, since I couldn't sit there and ignore the water
dripping off my chin. The handle moved again. "Go away,"
the Gaffer said sharply. "All right now?" he asked me.

I nodded, but held my breath in case.

He put one foot up on the rung of a stool and was quiet for
a long time. "I'm puzzled," he said at last. He stared at a
corner of the ceiling. "I'm very understanding and
generous, and I say, I'll let you off this time – and you bust
out crying!"

"I didn't," I said automatically, then bit my thumb and
tried to move a sweet-paper across the floor by will-power.

"Why, Gray? Just tell me that – why?"

I bit harder at my thumb. "I dunno," I said. "I dunno."

"Don't give me that, Gray."

I wasn't going to tell him why. Apart from the difficulty
and embarrassment of explaining why to anybody but
myself, the why was *mine*; I'd thought it out, and it was

going to stay mine. I gnawed round my thumb-nail, my eyes sliding around the office, desperately trying to think of some other explanation that would get me out of here.

"Get your dirty hands out your mouth," he said. I stopped biting my thumb, for the moment. He leaned back comfortably on the door. "Well?"

I couldn't think of anything but the truth; and he wasn't going to move until I said something, so I said, "It's nothin', Gaffer – honest – 's nothin'."

"You keep sayin' that – you can keep sayin' it all night for all I care. There must be some reason." He thought he was on to something. After all, my brother had left home, and did look like a hippy; and the police had to come and take me home. He'd never said anything about that after, but his curiosity must have been simmering away. Perhaps if he poked around long enough, he'd stir up something murky.

"You don't want to know – " I began.

"Yes, I do," he said.

"But you wouldn't be interested – it's saft, Gaffer – "

"So let me have a laugh."

I sighed jerkily. I supposed that if I sat here long enough, he'd have to give in. But I thought I'd probably go barmy first. "I was hopin' you'd sack me," I said. I looked up at him under my brows. I couldn't work out what he was thinking. "It was disappointment like, Gaffer. I couldn't help it, I'd been countin' on you sackin' me. I thought you would for sure. I thought after all I'd done it'd be Instant Dismissal, and I'd be finished today. I was tryin' for last Saturday – and then today you said – I thought you meant you was going to give me the sack – and then you said you was letting me off."

The Gaffer was staring at me, his brain slowly ticking away. "You mean all that being late and rude to customers was all deliberate – just to get the sack, I mean?"

I nodded.

He shook his head. He sniggered. "I never heard anything like it. You deliberately did all that – all this bad behaviour

127

everybody's been complaining about for weeks was you trying to get yourself the sack?"

"Yes," I said.

He nearly took me head off with his one hand as he went past me to sit at his desk. "Gray, you amaze me, you really do. Wouldn't it have been easier just to hand in your notice?"

"Me Dad wouldn't have liked it."

"You want to leave and your Dad doesn't want you to? You've been thinking of an outdoor job – was it you? Must have been. What's your Dad got against a nice, healthy, outdoor life?"

"He thinks I ain't old enough to decide whether to change me job or not."

"You was old enough to decide to get this job."

"It was me Dad told me to come for the interview, and to take this job."

"Oh," he said.

"And to go on the Manager Course," I said. "I wouldn't, left to meself. Too much like school, with the homework and that."

The Gaffer was quiet a minute, while he stared at me. "But you're doin' well, Gray. You'll pass the exam most likely, so I'm told. You work well here."

I shrugged. "I wouldn't have took the job of me own accord."

He said impatiently, "Why did you then?"

I shrugged. "I'd got nothin' else. An' Dad kept sayin' it was a good job, and go on, take it, and I knew he really meant he wanted me to take the job." I spread my hands. "I couldn't go sponging on 'em for any longer, could I? I'd been without a job for a fortnight, and me dole didn't keep me. Just about paid the milk-bill."

He sighed through his nose. "What am I supposed to do, eh? It's all very well for you and your Dad, fighting your – guerrilla war down on the Pleck Estate – what about me?"

128

I grinned. "Sack me," I said. "If you don't now, you'll have to in the finish."

"Is that a promise?"

I nodded.

"All right," he said. "Come in Friday for your wages and a cup of tea. Tell us how you get on."

I stood up. "I'm sacked then?"

"If you want, but I think you'd do better to give notice. You won't have to tell any future employers that you was kicked out then."

"I want to leave now though – thanks, Gaffer – I mean, Mr. Tibbs – thanks!"

"Get out of me sight," he said.

I ran down the steps, turned at the bottom. "I'll stop till half-past five, if you like."

"Just go on home."

So I ran upstairs and fetched me jacket. Downstairs I passed Mrs. Harris and Claz with glad cries of "I'm sacked!" I didn't stop to see what they made of it. I went out through the check-outs, answering their "Where d'you think you'm going?" with "I'm sacked!"

I hit the door with my shoulder and ran out, yelled up at the church clock, "I'm sacked!" and then ran past it, and over the hill, down to the bus stop. The bus was at the stop, but waited for me. My luck was in.

Now all I had to do was outface me Dad. He wasn't going to like it. Maybe he was too late to stop me leaving Bancroft's, but he still wasn't going to like it, and he could be very stroppy when he was put out. You could put him out and there'd be nothing right for weeks after. It even crossed me mind that it might end with me having to get out, like Derek.

But I was still up in the air over winning – as I thought of it – the first battle. I liked the feeling so much that I almost looked forward to the next round. I liked making my own way.

129

I wasn't going to leave home, and I wasn't going to fall out with Dad and end up fighting an endless quarrel out either. One or the other of us was going to have to change their ideas. My ideas were too new to change them yet. Or maybe we could sort of meet half way. Have a bit of tolerance about the house.

With luck.

6

Mother said, "Graeme! You'm early, love." I shouldn't have taken the first bus. I should have hung about a bit, and come on the one I usually take.

"Yeah," I agreed with her, as if it was nothing unusual. "Can I have summat to eat please, I'm hungry?" And off she went into the kitchen, just as I intended her to. I wondered if she knew that I'd meant her to, and had gone anyway. She called, "Hang up your coat, love, will you?"

"All right," I said. Anything to oblige and keep her quiet.

She didn't go on about my being early, and while I dipped digestive biscuits in me cup of tea, I pretended to be wrapped up in this old magazine, hoping she wouldn't disturb me. She didn't. Which was really a bit surprising. She didn't even start talking about television programmes, or neighbours, or people she'd met while shopping that used to live down our street. I couldn't help thinking that the reason she kept quiet was because she guessed. She knew what I'd done. I was frightened to look up in case she was watching me. Reading me like a book, as they say.

Dad came in and dinner was served. Mother didn't mention to him that I'd been early, which made it difficult for me to find an opening, and convinced me even more that she knew already. I kept looking across at him, and making and forgetting sentences. In the finish, I just said, "Dad, I've been sacked."

He stopped with his fork in his mouth. He took it out. "Eh? What you mean? You've been sacked? Bloody sacked? How've you been sacked? What have you been doin' to be sacked?"

"The Gaffer said me work wasn't satisfactory."

"Your work wasn't satis – wasn't satisfactory? Has it took him two years to find out your work wasn't satisfactory?"

He was accusing me, not the Gaffer. I hedged. "I dunno. He just said me work wasn't satis-factory and sacked me."

"Just like that." He snapped, "You've been there two years and he's never complained."

He waited for an answer. A confession. I suppose – a surrender. "No," I said. "He never has." I tapped a rhythm on the edge of my plate with my fork.

Dad glared at me. "What have you done to be sacked?"

"I don't know," I said. I looked up and stared back into his eyes. They were bright blue and angry. I don't know how eyes can be just eyes and angry at the same time.

Dad tapped his finger on the table. "You don't get sacked after two years for no reason at all. Why wasn't your work satisfactory?"

"It's just – " I tried to think of some reason it would be safe to give. I couldn't think of anything, I mean, not even the date of the Battle of Hastings. Mother put the tea-pot down and said, "Did he say he'd got the sack?" Dad gave her a vicious look. She can always be relied on to break up your concentration. Dad turned on me suddenly and yelled, nearly blasting me off me chair, "What did you do?"

I blinked, and jumped, but he made me mad. "Nothin'!" I yelled back.

His mouth opened and his bottom lip jutted out in a very comical way. He thumped the table and leaned across it, pointing his finger at my nose. "You tell me now, my lad, or I'll knock your bloody head off!"

I stood up from my chair, feeling very small and thin, but

132

hot as a live wire. "Whatever I did I ain't going to tell you, so – so drop dead!"

We stood there, staring into each other's eyes like summat off the telly, him as mad as fire, and me growing more and more worried, especially after I'd told him to drop dead. He knew I was lying, and he knew I wasn't going to admit. He made to shout again, but didn't, and I watched his anger die. He saw that whatever he said, whatever he did, and whatever laws he laid down, I was going to duck under 'em just as I'd done this time. He sat down solidly and said, "You crafty little bugger."

"Did he say he's been sacked?" Mother asked again.

"He's got hisself the sack," Dad said.

"Oh Graeme," she said, but without any particular expression.

I jumped to my own defence, tripping over words in anger and haste. "I know where I can get another job. I shall go for it tomorrow an' I shall get it, you'll see. And I'll stick it," I said to Dad.

"You'd better, my lad. *If* you get it."

"I'll get it."

"You'd better," he repeated, more loudly. "Because I'll tell you – I ain't keepin' you. You don't work, you don't eat in this house. I've got no time for bloody idle folk. Like your brother."

"I wish you'd keep your voice down, Dick. These walls are so thin," Mother said. Dad spun round in his chair and yelled at the wall, "Blow the bloody neighbours!"

I thought I'd get out of the way for a while. I went into the kitchen and fetched half a cup of water for my cactus. She was closing – she closed at night. I was proud of her though.

As I turned round, I saw a patch of something white under me bed. I bent down to see. It was my pile of dirty comics. I flipped through the pages. They were still frank and unexpurgated. All really was forgiven.

I went to the door and switched off the light. The hall was

in darkness. A line of light shone under the living-room door and the telly clamoured. The light in the kitchen was on, and I heard water running into a kettle. I decided to go and make contact before she took my porn again.

I crossed the hall into the kitchen, and went up behind her, put my arms round her waist and kissed the nearest bit of her, which happened to be her ear.

"What's that for?" she said. "What you after – I know you, cupboard-love."

"I ain't after nothin'."

She turned and hugged me, and stroked my hair. I felt a bit of a charlie. "It's a long time since I had a cuddle of you," she said. "You must have been six last time."

We leaned back from each other, arms still linked around each other's waists. "Is Dad mad?" I asked, since it was obvious she wasn't.

She smiled and pushed away the hair that hung in my eyes. "A bit. No, I don't think so, not much anyway." She giggled and whispered, "I think he's a bit tickled, matter of fact. 'Crafty little so-and-so' he says. Come here a bit." She hugged me and I hugged her, and we sort of swung backwards and forwards. After the embarrassment had worn off a bit it was warm and comfortable, smelling of soap-powder and fruit-cake; and, for me anyway, a bit exciting. We stood back laughing at each other.

"Here are," she said. She stopped, opened the dresser-cupboard and took out a cake in a brightly patterned box. "Jersey slice. I bought two, one for your Dad and one for us. Now you go and take him that."

I took the cake and went quietly into the living-room. He sat on the settee, and I dropped the cake into his lap. He didn't look up.

I glanced at the telly, and that dancing team was on – all them girls. I stood there staring, watching 'em stamp and wriggle and turn. There's this big, tall, broad-faced blonde with 'em that's my favourite. She's really great. I licked me lips and moved round to get a better view and Dad looked up and saw me. "Get to bed," he said.

"Eh?"

"Get to bed."

"It's only – "

"Get to bed."

I decided to treat it as a joke – I thought it might be. "Why is it the older generation always get nervous when there's summat sexy on the telly and a member of the younger generation about?"

I thought he was going to get angry again, but he grumbled out, "The older generation gets nervous waiting for the questions to start."

The dancing had finished and I moved further round the settee. "I don't need to ask questions, so you needn't worry."

"Oh no," he said, deep in his throat. "You know it all, don't you?"

I sat down on the floor by his knee, leaning me back against the settee's arm. "They teach it at school. In the fourth year, so you'm all ready for when you leave. All they don't tell you is what you really want to know."

"Thank God for small mercies anyroad," he said.

"Don't you reckon sex-education then, Dad?"

"If I'd asked my Dad that, he'd have knocked me head off. Here, fill your mouth with that instead of questions." He passed me down a piece of cake he'd broken off his own.

I looked back to the telly where these blokes were drinking and talking in a pub. It was supposed to be funny. Dad said, "I just hope you ain't going to be sorry." He drummed his fingers on the top of my head. "Bloody know-it-all. Got too much about you. Been too easy on *you*, I have. . . . Should have knocked it out on you years back." Then he laughed and pulled a single hair from the top of my head.

Ouch.

Other Faber Teenage Paperbacks

THE ROOM WITH NO WINDOWS
Gene Kemp

'Everything here is out of this world, though I'm not sure I fit in. Sometimes I feel as if I'm a raw onion being peeled, layer by layer till there's nothing left, especially if Harry picks on me. Sometimes I've got things to say but I'm scared to, for if I do, it sounds false or funny, peculiar not ha-ha, or someone else says something wittier or louder or cleverer and nobody hears me. But it doesn't matter because I can talk to Tass.'

Gene Kemp's third novel for teenagers describes a young girl's emotional turmoil as the holiday of a lifetime gradually turns into a nightmare . . .

'Kemp remains a first-rate storyteller.' Naomi Lewis, *Observer*

0–571–16117–0

JOSEPHINE
Kenneth Lillington

'Josephine Tugnutt was excusably nervous as she walked up the tree-lined avenue that led to St Chauvin's College. One girl among six hundred boys! She came from a girls' boarding school, and was walking into the unknown . . .'

It's 1932, the year of the great Yo-Yo craze, and St Chauvin's is another world altogether. What strikes Josephine as odd at first glance, appears even more so at a second. Why does the English master make such free play with his sword? Did the science master really turn a boy into a wolf? Is Fearless of the Fifth quite what he would wish one to believe? With a no-nonsense thoroughness that does not, however, rule out the possibility of romance, Josephine sets about putting things to rights – with hilarious results.

'A frothy, sophisticated treat.' Stephanie Nettell, *Guardian*

0–571–16118–9

ALMOST JAPANESE
Sarah Sheard

'Everything Japanese was magic. Sheepskin coats were magic. I'd spot a car like his and my heart would jump. In the grocery store, I heard a laugh just like his and I almost died. Everything that connected to him was absolutely sacred. My daily life was so ordinary it was painful.'

Emma is fourteen when she meets and falls hopelessly in love with the distinguished Japanese musician, Akira Tsutsuma. The problems caused by the age difference between her and Akira and the objections of her parents finally put an end to her obsession for a man, but not her love of life and all things Japanese.

'An exquisitely crafted story.' *The Times*

'A real find.' *Look Now*

0-571-14863-8

FAMILY FEELING
Gina Wilson

Families can be difficult even when they are your own. When they are not really your own they can be worse.

Alice Mather was thirteen when her widowed mother married Donald Spenser. He was divorced; his daughter Corinna was eight and his son Edwin fifteen. Corinna did not like her stepmother but she took to Alice – as long as Alice indulged her. The smallest sign of neglect and she would do her best to make trouble. As to Edwin, he hardly looked at Alice at first; but it was different later . . .

Gina Wilson is an exceptional writer for teenagers, and *Family Feeling* is both a dramatic account of dangerous shifts in family relationships and the story of tentative first love. All her novels for young people show her penetrating but sympathetic insight into teenage emotions.

0–571–16119–7

SUMMERS OF THE WILD ROSE
Rosemary Harris

Nell Dobell arrives at Innsbruck with her school choir, to sing in a music festival. At the station her party is greeted by a deputation from the Innsbruck choir, and Nell falls out of her carriage and straight-away in love with Franz Walter, who is welcoming her with a bouquet. It seems like an idyll, but this is 1937; Hitler is preparing to march into Austria and Franz is half-Jewish. What future can there be for him and Nell? This poignant novel tells the story of two summers separated by nearly thirty years and two very different romances.

'A marvellous love story, full of sunlight, music and terrible heartache.' Adele Geras, *New Statesman*

0–571–16323–8

SCARS
Anne Bailey

'He was there. He was always there in my mind. I hadn't spoken since it happened. I couldn't speak.' For two years, Tanya had stayed silent; all the sympathy of her family and the probing of the psychiatrists hadn't helped. Was it just the shock, or was she afraid of what she might give away if she spoke? *Scars* is both a convincing psychological study of a deeply injured girl and a gripping mystery.

Gene Kemp has said of this remarkable first novel by a young author: 'Her work is strong and spare, and describes attitudes which seem to me to be nearer to the truth than those often wished upon teenagers by older authors. *Scars* shows too how appalling experiences can be survived and end in optimism and hope.'

'Compulsive reading.' *Times Literary Supplement*

0–571–16322–x